FURRED LINES

Peculiar Mysteries Book 7

RENEE GEORGE

Barkside of the Moon Mysteries

FURRED LINES

Peculiar Mysteries Book 7

Cover Art: Renee George

Print February 4, 2018

ISBN-10: 194717715X

ISBN-13: 978-1947177154

ACKNOWLEDGMENTS

Dear Readers,

I have to thank you for wanting to hear Nicole's story. I adored getting know Sid Taylor and his wife Jean while exploring the unexplored parts of Peculiar. So I have to thank you for the kick in the pants.

For Robbin, thank you for always being there for me, even when you are too busy to breathe, you still make space for me. I should be kissing your ass every day. For Michele Bardsley for all her great edits, suggestions, and revisions. Also, for all her crazy good knowledge about psychopaths and serial killer. I am so glad you love me because I'm afraid of what might happen if you didn't.

Lastly, I have to thank my Rebel Readers. I ADORE you guys! Thank you for being loyal fans ((((hugs))). I also want to thank the Peculiar Fans for making this mystery romance series one of my best sellers! I will keep writing them as long as you want to keep reading them.

XXOO,
Renee George

Welcome to Peculiar, Missouri!

Wereraccoon Nicole Taylor, a recent Quantico graduate, is eager to prove herself. She's been assigned to work with oh-so-yummy field agent and werebear Dominic Tartan to catch a therianthrope serial.

Dom doesn't know what to make of the sexy recruit he's been tasked to train. Half the time he wants to ditch her, the other half of the time he wants to kiss her. Nicole struggles with the urge to sock him one or jump his bones.

Doomsday preppers, a dead body, and a crate full of stolen guns make the case even more Peculiar. Can Nicole and Dom find the killer in the chaos? Or will someone close to Nicole be the psycho's next target?

For my husband,
the Smokey to my Bandit.
I adore you.

CHAPTER ONE

I took a deep breath and straightened my collar. "I am an FBI agent," I said to myself in affirmation. "Special Agent Nicole Taylor and I've earned the right to be here. Nothing can take this away from me but me."

As I continued to mutter my new mantra, I assessed my outfit for the umpteenth time. I'm a therianthrope, a person who can turn into an animal. In my case, the animal is the *Procyon lotor*—you know, a raccoon. Fun fact about raccoons, their paws are extremely sensitive. Even in my human form, my hands and feet were crazy responsive. Thus... my choice of the black, riveted boots.

The stylish boots were formal enough for my black slacks, black faux-fur lined bomber jacket, and a dark blue button-down shirt, but had just enough rock-n-roll toughness to help me get away with my silver aviators. My black hair was pulled back into a severe ponytail. I wore little makeup other than some concealer under my eyes, which were naturally dark because, hel-lo, raccoon here, and a tiny bit of lip color. I checked out myself in the black sedan's side mirror and was satisfied I had successfully straddled the line of professionalism and vanity.

I noticed movement out of the corner of my eye and straightened to watch the man cross the parking lot at the Kansas City Field Office. I'd been told I would be assigned to a senior agent who had spent the past several years working undercover. I don't know what I'd expected, maybe a beard, rough hair, tattoos, and the edge of a thug. Instead, I got a man with a chiseled jawline, a perfectly aquiline nose, sharp cheekbones, firm sensuous lips, and the palest green eyes I've ever seen. I reached out to brace myself against the hood of the car, missed and tripped forward. My cute boots that had seemed like a good idea minutes before acted as a wedge when I tried to catch myself, and they sent me careening forward.

Right into Mr. Green Eyes's arms. I congratulated myself for not lingering over his bulging biceps as he assisted me into an upright position.

"Doctor Nicole Taylor?" he asked, his mouth tugged up at the corners in a wry smile. "You are Doctor Taylor, right?"

"Yes," I said when I'd swallowed enough spit to wet my dry throat. Jesus, this man was the eighty candles on my grandmother's last birthday cake. Hot, hot, hot. It was a fire I definitely needed to blow out, and no, that isn't a euphemism. This man was going to be my partner and mentor on my first big case. The bureau frowned on frater-nization in the ranks, and I had no plans to jeopardize my career before it got started. "You must be Special Agent Tartan."

He looked me over, and while he seemed amused, he didn't look all that impressed. "I read your file, Doctor Taylor. You have a Ph. D. in behavioral psychology." He shook his head. "And still, you chose to go to Quantico and join the FBI instead of private practice."

I crossed my arms so I wouldn't fidget. "That's right." I made direct eye contact and didn't allow my voice to waver. "And you have a bachelor's in criminology and twelve years of field experience. And, by your half-flirting half-condescending tone, I can tell you are attracted to me, but you don't think I'm cut out for the work, so you can't decide if you want to drop me straight away or sleep with me first and then get rid of me." I smirked as he stopped smiling. "I'm here to tell you, neither will happen. I'm not a horny teenager who can't keep it in her pants, and I'm a damn good agent."

"There is more to field work than test scores," Tartan said.

"And there's more to me than what you see," I countered. I'd always been on the shorter side, so he towered over me by at least nine inches. I didn't flinch under his heated gaze.

After a few seconds, he nodded. "We'll see."

"Yep." I nodded back.

We faced off for another few seconds until Tartan pulled his coat collar up and said, "Do you have the keys? Or are we going to stand in this cold parking lot all day?"

"Oh." The heat of a blush warmed my cheeks. It was

February in Missouri, and the temperature, which had been in the sixties yesterday, was in the thirties today. I dug the car keys from my pants' pocket and unlocked the door with the fob. "Where we off to?"

"Springfield," he said. "A man went missing two nights ago. We believe he is another victim of the guy the news is calling the Little Piggy killer."

Information about the serial killer taking the victim's pinky toes had been leaked to the press, and one reporter had used the nickname as clickbait to get people to read her article. It had worked, and unfortunately, the name caught on.

"No body?" I blinked in surprise. "The last three bodies have been placed near their homes within a week of going missing, right?" His M.O. had been all over the news the past six months since the third victim was found. "Do you think this guy is still alive?"

He opened the passenger side of the car. "Our job is to find out."

I frowned as he got inside and buckled up. Springfield was about two hours south of Kansas City. I got behind the wheel. "I'll take forty-nine highway to thirteen all the way down unless you want me to take a different route."

"You're driving," Tartan said. He pulled his phone wrapped with earbuds from his jacket and put the speakers in his ears. He gave me a sideways glance as he put his seat back. "Wake me when we get there."

"I'd hoped we could talk about the case on the way down."

My partner turned on some music, sort of a grungy-

4

blues tune I'd never heard. He cranked the volume then closed his eyes.

"I guess we aren't talking about the case," I muttered.

"Good guess," he muttered back.

My eyes widened. How in the world had he heard me over all that loud music? In an even quieter voice, I said, "Looks like Clark Kent. Hears like Superman."

He took the earbuds from his ears and stared at me. "You think I look like Clark Kent?"

I actually thought he looked more like Superman, the latest Henry Cavill version, but I had been trying to provoke him. "There's no way you could have heard me. And you weren't facing me so you couldn't have read my lips. Who are you? And even more to the point, what are you?"

He put his buds back in and leaned back. "I'm your partner, for now. Dominic Tartan. A black bear therianthrope. And you're Nicole Taylor, daughter of Sid and Jean Taylor, raccoon therianthropes." He opened one eye and smirked at my expression. "I guess you don't know everything about me, do you?" He gestured with his chin. "By the way, your dad told me to tell you hi, and that you should call your mom. She worries."

I started the car, my hands shaking as I pulled out of the parking space and got on the road. Dominic Tartan, the FBI agent assigned as my partner was a shifter? And how in the hell did he know my dad? I fought the urge to scream as I headed down Summit Street and away from our field office. This. Was. Not. Happening. My dad, the sheriff of Peculiar, had somehow managed to set me up.

As if on cue, my phone rang. I pulled it out of my pocket. A picture of my mom displayed on my screen with the option of red to decline or green to answer.

"You going to ignore that?" Dominic asked.

I tapped the red circle. "Yep."

It rang again. Ugh.

"Mommy issues?"

"You have a psychology degree?"

"Nope."

"Well, I do. So how about you let me worry about me, and you worry about you." I tapped the green button and put the phone to my ear. "Hi, mom." I plastered a fake smile on my face because my mother would hear the irritation in my voice otherwise. She might not be a psychologist either, but she could read people like no one I'd ever met before, and her intuition was off the charts. "Sorry I dropped your call. I was in the middle of something."

Dominic raised his brows at me.

"It's all right, puddin'. I'm just calling to see how your first day is going?"

"Oh, fine." I tried not to sound like I swallowed a bug. "Everything is A-okay."

"Well, that great. I'm glad to hear it."

I adjusted the phone between my shoulder and ear. "Did you need anything else, Mom?"

"Your dad says hi."

I glanced at Dominic. "That's what I hear."

The silence on Mom's end was deafening.

"I've got to go. Love you."

"Love you right back," she said and hung up.

I dropped my phone into the carrier in the car's console.

"You shouldn't drive while on the phone," Dominic said.

"Thank you for that public service announcement, Agent Tartan. My eyes have been opened, and you have changed my world. You're a hero."

A sound emitted from him that was a combination of grunt and snort. "You're welcome, *puddin'*."

One of the things I didn't miss about living in a town of therianthropes was the lack of privacy. In our human forms, we were a little stronger than humans, and our senses were more in tune with our surroundings. In other words, Dominic, as a werebear, who could hear my whispers over his loud music, had also listened to every word my mom had said to me. "Why was I assigned to you, Agent Tartan?"

"Call me, Dom." He scrolled through some files on his tablet.

I gripped the steering wheel tight enough to my knuckles white. "That's not an answer."

He shrugged. "Take the next exit. 71 South to 54 east to 13 south. That'll be the quickest route to Springfield."

I bit back a groan. "You know I grew up in the Ozarks. I've done some pretty extensive traveling between here and Springfield, so if you don't mind, I'll do my own navigating."

Dom chuckled. "Fair enough."

"Thank you."

"Did you get a chance to look through the files yet?"

"I was only given this assignment last night, but I did read through the first three murders." I wiggled my fingers while controlling the steering with my thumbs. They creaked with crepitus. I gave Dominic a cursory glance before turning on my left blinker and passing the eighteen-wheeler going sixty in a sixty-five. "He grabs his victims as they arrive home from work. He leaves no trace of himself behind, no DNA, fingerprints, hair, foreign fibers. There are no tire tracks leading to or from the abduction site. He's basically a ghost. He has spaced out his kills long enough that it took a while for the police to connect the cases. The first two victims were six months apart, and the third one eight months after that, then four months on this one. There doesn't seem to be a pattern to his killing. Within a week after the abduction, he places the body somewhere the family can find it. They always have a pinky toe missing, which the media has picked up on, and they are tortured with some kind of sharp implement. Oh, and he cuts off their pinky toes for some reason." I could have recited the files word for word since I had an eidetic memory, but I found it creeped most people out when I put that ability on display. "Did I leave anything out?"

"This fourth case is the one you should have read."

I passed two more vehicles and settled back into the right lane of traffic. "Why's that?" I hadn't been given the fourth case to review.

Tartan held his phone screen up at an angle to show me a picture he'd pulled up on the screen. I was confused as I looked at a punch card with six paw prints punched out of twenty-eight tiny squares, and in the middle of the card was a bear logo with the words Blonde Bear Cafe Loyalty Card.

A wave of nausea washed over me.

"You know what this is, right?" Dom asked.

"Sure, it's a card from Blondina Messers' restaurant. I probably have one of those in my wallet. Once you buy twenty-eight meals, you get a free lunch or dinner. Are you telling me that was taken from the crime scene?"

"Don't have a heart attack, Agent Taylor. Your dad confirmed that the latest victim doesn't live in Peculiar. And appears to never have visited, either."

"The killer is a therianthrope?" Even though I was an FBI agent, I worked on the human side of the law. Suddenly it was perfectly clear why I'd been assigned to Dominic Tartan. This serial killer wasn't a human psychopath. Shit. We were looking for a shifter. "All the victims were shifters?"

"Yes." He looked at the tablet. "And this card proves the killer is familiar with your hometown."

I shook my head. "The killer can't be anyone from Peculiar. It's just not..." I shook my head again. "No."

"That card was found near the victim's front porch. It's got a gloss surface, so prints have been pulled, and they are running them through forensics," Dom said. "You wanted to know how we were partnered up? Well, Agent Taylor, I requested you."

"Because I'm from Peculiar?"

"Yes, that and it's an in. You know what these therianthrope towns are like. They are pretty closed up with integrators like me, and no human is going to be allowed to

9

get in there to investigate. Your dad said we can work out of his office. We're going to check in with the locals in Springfield, get up to speed on the current victim, and then we are going to take our investigation to your hometown."

My knuckles were white again as I turned on to the 54-highway exit. "Great. Fun, fun." I guess I was going home.

CHAPTER TWO

*W*e arrived in Springfield after a lot of silent car driving. I pulled into the parking lot of the FBI office on Chesterfield and parked near the front doors.

"We'll coordinate with an Agent Dale Resnik," Dominic said. "He's a good guy. I've worked with him once before a couple years back."

"So, he's a therianthrope?"

"Nope." Dom shook his head. "He's human. Completely unaware, and that's the way we have to keep him and every other human we run into on this case. That's part of our job."

"For the FBI?"

"No, for the Tri-State Council."

I groaned. "What have they got to do with this?" I'd heard all about the fiasco at the Tri-State Council meeting two years ago when Peculiar had been picked to host the event. Two deaths and a kidnapping had occurred that week as a result. If it hadn't been for the two newcomers in town, Chavvah Trimmel and Sunny Haddock, the killers might have kept on their spree. I didn't know either lady very well.

"We work for the FBI, Nicole, but as therians, we're in a position to help our kind. Do you know what would happen if humans found out about us?"

"I have a fair idea, Mr. Patronizing." I'd thought many times of ways that our kind might fully integrate into human society. "But would it really be that awful? After all, there are many of us who protect humans every day, military, doctors, nurses, EMTs, firefighters, and law enforcement. If we were allowed to perform to our fullest abilities, we could show them that we are assets, not enemies."

"It's naïve to think that humans as a whole are going to embrace our otherness. People, even our own kind, tend to fear the unknown, and we would be feared by many. All that aside, until the powers that be deem it time to come out of our metaphorical furry closets, do you really want humans to find out about us by accident? Like if a shifter murderer, kidnapper, rapist, or thief was the reason our species was placed in the spotlight."

"That would be bad."

Dom smiled. "Is that your clinical opinion?"

"My clinical opinion is that the man is intelligent and organized."

"And what makes you think it's a man?"

"All the victims have been therianthropic men whom our unknown subject has somehow subdued. This last one put up a struggle, and still, the unsub was able to take him down. I've known some pretty strong women, and if these were human victims, I'd say it could go either way, but our kind is harder to take down." I shook my head. "We're definitely looking for a male. Someone aged twenty-six to upwards of sixty." Therianthropes aged much slower than humans. We still died of old age, but old age tended to occur after one-hundred twenty years, and we could potentially live to be one-hundred and eighty to two-hundred years before dying of natural causes. "I'll need more information than what's in the files to discern more. Also, I think we should look over the past two to three decades to see if this kind of thing has happened before. If we could find more victims, that will give us even more information about his age."

"Good idea," Dom said.

"Thanks. I have one or two every now and then." I smiled.

"You also have a really nice smile."

I blinked, dumbstruck over the out-of-the-blue compliment. I frowned. "Stop flirting with me." I took the key out of the ignition. "We should go in."

Dom grinned, his gray-green eyes sparkling like polished jade. "I'll follow you in a moment. I need to make a call."

The FBI offices were located in a building that shared space with an investment company called Truman & Associates. Big letters near the entrance marked the company as important. There was no similar signage for the FBI field office.

When I walked into the field office, I was startled to

RENEE GEORGE

see a familiar face talking with a middle-aged man in a gray suit.

"Eldin?" I asked.

Eldin Farraday, a tall guy, with a thin, but handsome face, smiled warmly as he recognized me. "Nic!" He came around the desk where he was standing, pushed his way past swinging door by the front counter and swept me up in his arms. His affectionate hug nearly broke my spine. "What the hell are you doing here?"

"I was assigned to the Little Piggy case," I told him when he set me back down on the floor. He still had his arms around me, and I pressed my ear against his chest and listened, familiarly, to the sound of his heartbeat. I sagged against my friend. "Damn, it's good to see you."

"Deputy Farraday," Dominic said, his voice low and what I could only describe as grouchy. "Did Sheriff Taylor send you?"

"He thought I might be able to help," Eldin said, his arms still around me. "I didn't know Nic was coming, though. If I had, I'd have worn her favorite cologne."

I leaned back and beamed up at him. "I don't like Fahrenheit that much," I lied.

He kissed me quickly on the mouth, a light peck. "I've missed you, Nic. You don't come home often enough."

"I've missed you too." I pulled away from Eldin's embrace.

The blond-haired man, who I assumed was Agent Resnik, smiled at me. "You greet all your colleagues that way? If so, where do I line up?"

"No, she doesn't," Dom answered as he stiffly passed

Eldin and me to greet the agent. "How are you, Resnik?" he said to the man as he held out his hand.

"Good, Tartan. You?"

"Real good." I watched as Dominic shook off whatever bug had crawled up his butt to paste on his charming smile. "The hugger is my partner, Nicole Taylor."

I walked to the back and shook Resnik's hand. "Sorry about that. Deputy Farraday and I grew up together. He's an old friend."

"I need to get new friends," the blond said, his smile widening. "I hope you guys can shed some light on this case. I've hit a dead end, and this one hasn't followed the same pattern as the others. I'm not even sure it's the same guy."

"How so?" Dom asked.

"Well, for one, evidence was left behind. For another, the guy's body hasn't shown up yet."

"I can't believe anyone in Peculiar has anything to do with this, Agent," Eldin said to Resnik.

When I was a child I might have agreed, but I wasn't a child anymore, and our small town had had enough of its fair share of crime over the past two decades for me to believe it was possible. Unfortunately, therians were just like humans when it came to greed, lust, and revenge. Luckily, they also had the same capacity for humor, kindness, and love.

"Honestly," Resnik said. "I'd never even heard of Peculiar until this case, and I've been assigned to the Ozarks for a decade now."

Not hearing about an all shifter town was by design.

Peculiar worked hard to stay off the radar. Which is why there was only one road in and out of town—no through traffic from one destination to another. If you were going to Peculiar, it had to be by design or pure accident. The fact that this case was drawing attention to the place probably scared the crap out of my dad.

Oh. Dominic hadn't requested me on the case, my father had. I glared at my partner. He shrugged and gave me the "what?" eyebrow raise.

"Later," I mouthed. "Agent Resnik, what can you tell us about the abducted man?"

Resnik took us to a corkboard with pictures from the current and previous abductees and their corresponding small toes, the Blonde Bear Café's loyalty card, a footprint, a broken porch rail with four large scratches, and some droplets of blood.

"Any of that blood from the suspect?"

"No." Resnik rubbed a hand through his hair. "Blood belongs to the vic. Bloody nose, we suspect, there was some mucus in the sample."

Neither Dom, Eldin, nor I asked about the scratch marks on the rail.

Resnik tapped the third man's picture. "Our newest victim. Ray Lieberman. President of Lark Manufacturing, a company that makes stainless steel appliances. Wife. Five kids and another on the way. Married twenty years, no prior legal problems. Solid guy as far as we can tell."

"Any enemies?" Dominic asked.

"Nope."

"Do you think he's dead?"

Eldin raised his chin. "You think he's not?"

"There's a struggle and no body." I looked at Resnik. "Any fingerprints on the card?"

"Several, but no hits, which means he doesn't have a record." The blond agent shrugged. "We're flying blind here without a map."

I looked at Dominic. "What next?"

"You go to Peculiar with Deputy Farraday." His expression soured as he gave me the directive. "I've got some business I have to take care of here in Springfield."

"Do you want me to stay and help?"

"It's personal, not professional."

"Oh." I handed him the keys. "See you later."

"I'll join you in Peculiar this afternoon. Line up some accommodations for us when you get there."

"I'll get you a hotel room at the Peculiar B & B. If I know my mom, my bed at home is already made-up." I glanced at Eldin. "Looks like it's you and me," I said.

"Just like old times." He grinned.

Dominic scowled. "Coordinate with the sheriff and try to remember that you're there on official business. This isn't a coming home party."

I stared him straight in the eye. "You obviously don't know my mother."

CHAPTER THREE

"*I*t's so great to see you, El. How's your folks?"

His father had been ill with Fox Flu the last time I'd been back. It was an ailment that affected, well, foxes, and other species that are close kin. The virus affected muscles and nerves in fox shifters, and sometimes, it affected smooth muscles, like the intestines and lungs. When it did, it was usually a death sentence. My mom had told me a couple of months back that Mr. Farraday had finally shaken the illness and was on his way to getting his life back to normal. I'd said a big thank you to the universe.

Eldin Farraday had once been my sweetheart in high school. My first love, so to speak, but other than some kissing and heavy petting in the back seat of his mother's van our senior year, our relationship hadn't amounted to much. Still, I'd always seen him as an ideal mate. Sweet, strong, and loyal. Those were qualities not easy to come by these days. And I still cared about him.

"Dad's doing much better. He's still weak in the legs,

and he's working on getting his grip strength back, but the physical therapy is going well, and Doc Smith said he should make a full recovery over time."

"Well, if Doc says he's on the mend then I believe it." I reached over squeezed Eldin's hand. He looped his fingers in mine and gave me a squeeze back.

"Thanks for asking, Nic." He took his hand back and put it on the steering wheel. "So, you're a big FBI agent now, huh? That's pretty exciting," he said, changing the subject.

"Yep, that's me. Big."

Eldin chuckled, and the warmth of his humor wrapped me up like a cozy blanket. "I've missed you, Nic. You should come home more often."

"I get home plenty," I said.

"As long as a federal crime is involved."

"Well, that's a given." I shook my head. "Though technically, I was doing a favor for my aunt last time. It wasn't an official case." I gave Eldin a light punch on the shoulder. "You know, I've missed you too. We didn't get much time to visit the last time I was home."

"I'm sorry about your aunt." He shook his head. "I know she was an unpleasant woman. God knows, she could try the patience of a saint, but she didn't deserve what happened to her."

I shrugged. Evelyn Meyers never met a person she couldn't piss off but, for whatever reason, I'd come running when she asked me to investigate her neighbor Milo Green. I still can't believe my dad thought I might be involved in Aunt Evelyn's murder. "She wasn't the kind of person to let you in," I told Eldin, "but still, my mom lost her sister, and that means something."

"What do you want to do first when we get to town? Check in with your mom or your dad?"

"We better see Dad first. I don't want to get off on the wrong foot with the local law enforcement." The corner of my mouth tugged up in a smile I couldn't hide.

"Your dad about blew a vein when he found out you'd joined the FBI."

"Believe me. I brought an umbrella for that conversation."

Eldin glanced at me, his brow raised.

"You know, for the blood spray."

He laughed. "Smart girl. But then, you've always been smart."

"Says the guy who used to cheat off my math homework."

"I always changed it just enough so Mr. Peters wouldn't suspect." He grinned.

Less than an hour of small talk about high school and the good ol' days later, Eldin pulled his police cruiser into a parking spot outside the sheriff's station.

"Time to face the music," I said.

Eldin hummed the Jaws' theme song as we exited the vehicle. Tyler Thompson walked out of the station as we were headed inside.

"Hey, Nicole," he said. "Good to see you."

I nodded my head. "You too."

The sheriff's station smelled like mildew, copier ink, and stale coffee. The crime board, as I'd called it when dad would take me to work with him, only had one open case on it, a reported theft at the Paw-On Pawn Shop on Main Street.

My dad sat behind his desk in his office, the dark circles under his eyes darker than normal, even for a raccoon shifter. He rubbed his temples. His shoulders slumped forward as if he carried the weight of the entire town on his shoulders. I guess in a way, he did. I fought back the impulse to crawl onto his lap like I had when I was small. Instead, I knocked on the frame of his open door.

"Hey, Dad."

His eyes slowly pivoted up and met my gaze. He gave me a tired smile. "Hey, kiddo. Come on in."

I sat in the chair across from him. "Are you okay?"

He shooed away my concern. "Fine, fine. Just got off the phone with Stenson. He's threatening to send a representative if we don't clear up this mess."

President Stenson, the new Tri-State Council President, had a bug up his butt about my dad since my Aunt Evelyn's case. Stenson had been having an affair with Evelyn, and he felt that my dad had mishandled the investigation. Which he had, but in his defense, he'd thought he was protecting me. Still, all therianthropes in the Missouri, Arkansas, and Kansas area were subject to the law of the council. They were our system of government, and Stenson had the authority to interfere if he wanted to take it that far.

"We'll just have to clear things up before that happens," I said.

Dad smiled. "That's my girl." He rubbed his face. "Darling, there hasn't been any disappearances in over three years."

"This isn't like then, Dad. No one is selling therians to hunters for sport."

"No, there is just some sick bastard, who apparently frequents our town, possibly someone we know, and who is carving people up and chopping off toes."

"Just one toe."

Dad shook his head. "That's not funny."

"Not even a little bit," I agreed.

"Stop it."

"I'm only the tiniest bit ashamed."

My dad leaned forward and tried to stare me down. "Little girl, I can still take you over my knee."

From the door, Eldin said, "Can I watch?"

At the same time, Dad and I said, "Shut up, Eldin." Then we locked gazes again. I cracked first. I laughed as I looked away. I could never beat my dad in a stare-off.

"Your mom is expecting you," Dad said.

"I need to get up to speed on any evidence you all have gathered then get a room at the motel for Agent Tartan." I already figured out my mother would not abide me getting a motel room. I wasn't even going to argue about it.

"Nonsense." Dad stood up and pulled the creases out of the trousers before he walked over to his coffee maker and refilled his cup. "Tartan can take the guest room."

Wait. What? I felt a mild sense of panic at the idea of Dominic staying at my parents' house. With me. Ack! "I don't think Dom would be all that comfortable there."

"Oh, you don't, do you? Go on and call your mother. Tell her you want to break her number one rule about hospitality."

Dang. He had me there. "You've been married to mom for too long," I groused.

"There will never be enough years for me."

My heart softened, and a small sigh of resignation escaped. "Fine. We'll stay at the house." In a way, I was glad. I still had clothes at home, and I'd only packed enough clothes for a couple of days. Which had been dumb, considering I had no idea how long this case would last. "But, just so you know, this is a federal investigation, Dad. We have to follow the FBI protocols."

"Look at her all grown up," Eldin said.

"Deputy Farraday," Dad said. "Don't you have work to do?"

"Uhm, yes, Sheriff. Getting on it." Eldin smirked and gave me a quick salute before he hustled back to his desk.

I turned my attention back to Dad. "Any leads about Little Piggy?"

Dad's exasperation was written on his face. "Not a gol-darn clue. I haven't had a chance to question Blondina, Roger, Selena, and Brandon. Farraday is running the prints against those of anyone we've arrested here in town, but so far I've got nothing."

"Brandon is back in town?"

"Yeah, after he got out of the Army, he struggled a little. Blondina and Roger talked him into coming back home."

That's good. I'm glad Brandon's back." Brandon Messer

had been a nice guy in high school, even if he had a little temper, but what hormonal teenage therianthrope didn't. He was an all-around athlete, good student, and he and Donna Kurts had been the prom King and Queen our senior year.

"Did he and Donna ever get married?"

Dad shrugged. "No. Brandon married a gal who was also in the Army. An integrator. Things didn't work out. Another reason his parents wanted him home. Donna married Brett Johnson. He owns the feed store outside of town."

"I remember Brett." He was older than Donna, who was my age, by about ten years, but in therian terms, an age difference wasn't that noticeable until a shifter got closer to one-hundred-years-old. "Isn't he related to the Delbert and Elbert?" The twin opossum shifters ran the general store in town. When I was young, the two men used to give me candy whenever dad or mom took me into their store.

"Distant cousin," Dad said. "Anyhow, when you interview the Messers, I'd like you to take Farraday with you. I think they won't be so nervous to give witness statements to people they know and trust. Agent Tartan agrees with me."

"Oh, you and Tartan agreed, huh? I love how I was included in the decision-making process. I'm not a lackey, you know."

"No, but you are his subordinate."

"In what world?" I asked.

"In the FBI, or am I missing something? Agent Tartan is a senior officer, isn't he?"

"He...I..."

Dad smiled as I fumbled with a defense. "So if you had been included, what would you have wanted to do?"

I slouched down in my chair feeling as grouchy as I must have looked. "I would have suggested that I interview the Messers without Tartan so they would be relaxed and be more willing to open up about their customers.

Dad nodded. "That's a good instinct, girl. I say you run with it."

I stuck my tongue out at him. "Gee, thanks, Sheriff. I'll do just that." I stood up and grabbed my purse. I walked over to my dad and kissed his cheek. "I'll see you at home, old man."

"Hey, now. Watch the old talk."

I smiled as I walked out of his office. I pointed my index finger at Eldin who had been pretending to do work. "You coming or what?"

CHAPTER FOUR

*M*y mother, for all her pride, had never been a perfect housekeeper. There was usually flour dusting the baking cabinet, the occasional spider web at a corner in the ceiling, and my dad's rolled up dirty socks by his easy chair. Still, she keeps a tidy house, and it always smells of strawberries—my dad's favorite scent.

Mom's car, a white luxury four-door, was parked in the driveway. Even from Eldin's cruiser, I could hear Aerosmith blaring from the house.

"Your mom is baking," he said, the smile on his face wistful. He'd spent a lot of time at my house when we were teenagers, so he knew Mom's habits as well as anyone.

I smiled. "I love it when she plays Aerosmith."

Eldin laughed. "Remember when she had us help her make that holiday bread for every person at the Silver Fox Senior Center? Four straight days of *Walk This Way*." His eyes went distant at the memory. "That is maybe my favorite memory of all time."

I smacked his arm. "Don't get all sentimental on me."

He met my gaze. "Would I do that?" He leaned over and kissed my cheek. "Can I take you to dinner tonight? There's something I'd like to talk to you about."

My throat tightened. Eldin and I had been sweethearts in high school. He'd been my first real love, but we'd agreed to see other people when I'd gone off to college. He was still so cute, but my feelings for him had changed from romantic to platonic over the years.

I touched his cheek, trying to hide my apprehension, and if I was honest, sadness. "Eldin..."

He put his hand over mine. "Don't worry, Nic. I'm not going to declare my intentions for you."

The tension in me eased, but the sadness remained. "Okay. I'll have to coordinate with Agent Tartan, but I'll figure it out. You want to meet at the Blonde Bear Café? We can kill two birds with one stone."

"If you really think I'm a bird that needs stoned."

I smacked him again. "I'll see you tonight."

THE HOUSE I GREW UP in was a two-story log house on forty acres of property replete with a small barn and full of country charm. The newer double pane storm windows my parents had put in two summers ago rattled as Steven Tyler commanded his audience, "to shut up and dance."

I walked in, because knocking would have kept me on the porch, and besides, no matter how long I'd been away, this old house in the woods would always be my home.

The entryway featured hardwood floors. My father had hand-sanded and laid the planks of dark walnut. I squatted and dragged my fingertips across the buttery surface. Each board in the floor had been a love letter to my mom. I stood up, feeling the beat of the music as I danced through the living room and took a left into the kitchen. Mom's usually neat hair, black but laced with silvery threads, was tied loosely back and long strands clung to her sweaty face as she punched and kneaded a basketball-sized round of dough.

She tilted her head back, flour dotting her cheeks, and tried to blow an unruly wisp of hair that had floated into her face. Her eyes locked on me for a moment before she let the dough go, threw her hands up in the air, and exclaimed, "Pixie, music off!" The room went silent.

"Nic! You're home." She came around the center island quicker than I could react and threw her arms around me.

"Mom," I whined. "You're getting me covered in flour."

She let go and observed the white powder now dusting my black jacket and slacks. She wrinkled her nose as her gaze studied me from head to toe. "That's what the washing is for." And on that note, she embraced me again. Since I knew there was no fighting it, I hugged her back.

"What are you making?" I asked, keeping my fingers crossed for cinnamon rolls.

"I've got the butter warming and the cinnamon and sugar out, so what do you think?"

I danced up on my tip-toes. "Yum." I looked at the blue square box on her counter by the toaster and nodded. "I'm so glad you use the Pixie."

"Well, you see," she said, putting her arm around my shoulders. "My very smart daughter gave it to me as a Christmas present."

"So you like it?"

"Oh my gosh, yes. Watch this." She faced the box. "Pixie, how many teaspoons are in a cup?"

The light on the top of the box blinked then it said, "One cup equals forty-eight teaspoons."

My mother grinned. "That contraption has made cutting recipes down so easy, plus it can do multiple timers, tell me the weather, and play my favorite music. I don't know how I managed without it." She squeezed me again before taking up her station in front of the dough ball.

It made me happy that mom loved my gift. It's like buying someone a sweater then catching them wearing it. "It's really good to be home."

"I'm so glad to see you," Mom said as she continued her kneading. "Your dad's missed you."

"So much he had to arrange for me to come home," I muttered.

Mom's expression flattened. "This business with Blondina's card ending up at a crime scene is attracting a lot of unwanted attention on the town, young lady. You know as well as I do that we can't have just anyone traipsing in and out of Peculiar. You should be flattered that your father arranged for it to be you."

Her sharp tone made me feel sixteen again. "It's hard to feel flattered when I'm feeling managed," I retorted. "I'm not a kid anymore. You and dad need to recognize that I can make my own decisions about my life."

Mom punched down the dough hard enough that her knuckles rapped the butcher block underneath. She winced as she looked at her hand. The middle knuckle was bleeding. She picked up the entire wad of dough and threw it in the trash. "I have to start over now," she said as she washed her hands in the sink. "You take your bag up to your room and get settled. We'll talk later."

A sourness settled in my stomach at her dismissal, but I'd learned long ago, that there was no talking to Jean Taylor when she was angry.

"Fine," I said, grabbing my small case. I practically ran up the stairs to my room and slammed the door behind me. Gah! The second I was alone in my room, I hated myself. Why did I always devolve into a petulant child around my parents? I could cite several psychological theories on the matter, but the truth was, my parents were supportive, loving, and they encouraged me to go live my life independently of them. I had no good reason for feeling, for lack of a better phrase, "picked on."

My phone rang, thank heavens, and took me out of the stew I'd been boiling in. I didn't recognize the number, but I answered anyhow. "Hello."

"Nicole?"

I recognized the voice. "Agent Tartan."

"Where are you?"

"I'm at my parent's house."

"Oh. Were you able to book me a room at the motel?"

"No," I told him. "You've been booked into the Taylor Home for Wayward FBI Agents. We have a guest bedroom downstairs, and Mom insists on putting us up while we're in town."

"Hmmm. I'd rather we stay at the local hotel to prevent distractions."

While I'd been irritated at my mom a few minutes earlier, I managed to shift that feeling to Dominic. "I'm staying at my parents' place. You can go un-distract yourself where ever you like."

"No, no," he said, his tone placating. "I just thought...well, it doesn't matter. Text me the address, and I'll be on my way in an hour or so..."

I hung up without saying goodbye and grudgingly texted him. Next, I added his number to my contacts under the name "Agent Pain in My Ass."

My phone rang as I stared at my handiwork. I fumbled to answer. "Hello. Er, I mean, Agent Taylor here."

"Agent Taylor," Eldin said on the other side. "How about lunch?"

My stomach gurgled in response. "I could eat."

CHAPTER FIVE

The Blonde Bear Café smelled of grilled burgers, French fries, and today's special, hearty chicken noodle soup. In other words, yummy. My stomach growled.

"Someone's hungry," Eldin said as we scanned the busy restaurant.

"You should have been a detective, deputy." I patted my belly. "You missed your calling."

"How about we maybe poke around while we're here?"

"You're twisting my arm."

A tall, broad woman with platinum blonde hair done up in a beehive and leathery tan skin came out of the back. Her smile split her face when she saw me. "Nicole, as I live and breathe, sugar. It's so good to see you home. You and Eldin grab yourself an empty table." She glanced around at the full house. "If you can find a spot."

"Over here!"

I turned to the voice and saw Sunny Trimmel and her sister-in-law Chavvah. Sunny was pointing to the two empty seats at their table. They were both newcomers to Peculiar, but my folks liked them, and even more of an endorsement, my dad trusted them. Still, there was something about the Mayor's wife that made me uncomfortable. I waved. "That's okay. We'll wait for a table to open up."

"Don't be ridiculous," Sunny declared. "You'll be waiting forever. Get on over here." She stood up, and I worried she planned to drag me over if I didn't comply."

Eldin leaned to my ear. "I've found that arguing with Sunny is a losing proposition."

I clenched my jaw, forced a smile, and said, "Fine," through gritted teeth.

Sunny moved over a chair so that she was across from Chavvah. That put Eldin and me across from each other. "Hey, Ladies. Enjoying your afternoon?"

Chavvah nodded. "Sure are."

Our waitress, Blondina's daughter Selena, placed menus down on the table. "How you all doing today?" Her ruffled apron looked like she'd stuffed it with a basketball.

"Good," we all answered in some variation of the polite response.

"Great." She pulled out a pad with paper and said. "Let me get your drink order going while I give you a chance to check out the menu."

"I'll have some sweet tea," Sunny said. Chav ordered unsweetened ice tea, Eldin a Dr. Pepper, and I ordered a coffee and ice water.

"It's been a long day," I explained.

When Selena left to fill our drink order, Chavvah asked, "How's the investigation going?"

My mouth dropped open. I closed it. I looked at the two ladies.

"My husband is the mayor. There's not much I don't know," Sunny explained.

Chavvah shrugged. "And her husband is my brother, so...."

"Besides, even if Babe wasn't her bro, I tell Chav everything." Sunny smiled.

"I'm not allowed to talk about an ongoing investigation, ladies. Sorry."

Sunny leaned in conspiratorially. "Okay. But can you tell us when we can expect the scrumptious Dominic Tartan to arrive? I really thought you all would come to town together."

A flush of warmth filled my cheeks. I avoided eye contact with Eldin. "Agent Tartan is on the way here. We are splitting up duties to gather as much information as we can."

Sunny leaned back in her chair and crossed her arms over her chest. "I know a certain doctor who isn't happy that the babe-alicous bear is making his way back here." Sunny wiggled her eyebrows in Chavvah's direction.

The brunette woman rolled her eyes. "You're dumb."

"Those dreamy green eyes, those soft brown curls." Sunny faked a swoon. "That fine, fine ass."

"You got more?" Chavvah said, not rising to the bait.

"I'd love to hear more," I interrupted. "What was it in particular that you liked about Agent Tartan's ass?" I thought if I pushed her, she'd get embarrassed and back off.

I was wrong.

"Why, Nicole, I'm so glad you asked." Sunny leaned forward and put her elbows on the table. "His bootie has the shape of two ripe cantaloupes attached to two thick tree trunks. I bet I could skip rocks on those rounded muscles." She shaped her fingers like grabby claws. "They just make a girl want to reach out and—"

"Got it," I said, leaning way back.

"I could go on," Sunny replied.

"And she will," Chav added.

"I'm sure you could." But I hoped she wouldn't.

Eldin started laughing. Even the stoic Chavvah cracked a smile.

Sunny giggled. "You're so easy, girl. This started as a way to tease my friend here, but you've made it too easy for me to redirect."

"That's me. Easy."

"Not that I recall," Eldin said.

"Ooooo," Sunny crooned. "Now this is getting more and more interesting as the conversation unfolds." She turned to Eldin. "What exactly do you recall about Nicole?"

I groaned. "Eldin hit his head when he was in high school." I glared a warning at him. "A lot. He has some memory loss."

He nodded. "Sudden onset."

Selena came back with our drinks balanced precariously on a round tray. She expertly set them down on the table.

I greedily picked up the coffee she'd set in front of me. I took a sip, and it was hot, hot. I put a cube of ice from my water in it. "Hey, Selena. I heard your brother is back in town."

The waitress bobbed her pretty head. "He sure is. I'm happy he's home, especially now that I'm pregnant again. He's a great uncle. Oof," she said. Her free hand rested on her stomach. "That was a hard kick."

Sunny absently put her hand on her own stomach. "I remember how hard those babies kick. You should take it easy."

Selena smiled. "Doc says I'm fine to work. I'm healthy as a bear."

"How far along are you?" I asked.

The waitress perked up at the chance to talk about her pregnancy. "Three months. Only two left. I can't believe how fast it's going. Michael is more anxious than I am."

Eldin nodded. "I can attest to that. It's always baby this and baby that at work."

Selena was married to Michael Connelly, one of my father's deputies. The pairing had surprised the hell out of me when my mother had called with the news. I'm not sure it was unprecedented, but I'd never heard of a squirrel and a bear therian mating before. The result would be interesting.

"Congratulations," I said. "Is this your first?"

"Second," Selena said. "Sunny predicted six kids for Michael and me."

I glanced over at Sunny who looked pleased. "She did, did she?"

Selena nodded. "She's never wrong."

Chavvah coughed. "Yeah, right."

"All right," Sunny said to her friend. "I'm wrong plenty. Just ask my husband." Her expression soured. "Actually, don't ask him."

"Well, you've never been wrong about me. You told me my ex was a cheating jerk, and you were right, and you told me I'd find love with Michael, and I did, and we are already well on our way to a house full of kids," she said with some indignation. She jerked her thumb at her chest to emphasize her next sentence. "If anyone says that you aren't anything but awesome, you send them my way."

"You hear that, Chav." Sunny beamed. "I'm awesome."

"I've known that for a long time," she said. "But I worry that if your head gets any bigger, it won't fit through the neck holes in your shirts."

Sunny grinned, her bright green eyes sparkled. "I know how to use a pair of scissors."

Selena chuckled. "Are y'all ready to order?"

"I'll take the open-faced roast beef sandwich piled high with mash potatoes and extra brown gravy," a man behind me said. I whipped my head around hard enough to wrench my neck. Dominic Tartan stood a few feet away. He raised his brow at my unasked question. "I finished up early in Springfield. Thought I would join you for lunch."

I'd texted him about my plans, but I didn't think he'd track me down.

He turned his gaze to the table, and his expression brightened immensely when he saw Chavvah. "Well, hello, Chav. Is it still Trimmel, or has the good doctor nailed you down yet?"

"He nails me every chance he gets," she said as if she

were commenting on the weather. The slight uptick of the corner of her mouth and the way she reached up to move a lock of hair from her shoulder told me she didn't mind the flirting, but I'd seen her with Doctor Smith, and if Tartan thought he had a chance in hell with the tall, leggy brunette, he was sorely mistaken.

"So not married." Dominic smiled.

"We've set a date," she said.

"March twentieth," Sunny said. "The Spring equinox or some such nonsense. Werewolves are a pain in the ass."

"True story," Chav said, "and they sure know how to ruin a perfectly good party."

Dom spread his hands. "Well, if it's a party you want..."

Selena, who had been waiting patiently for our orders, giggled.

I stood up. "There isn't room at this table for another chair. Agent Tartan and I will take the one Mr. And Mrs. Smart just left."

Selena's smile grew tight. "I'll get it cleaned up for you two." She looked at the deputy. "Should I make it for three?"

I said, "yes," while Dominic said, "no."

Eldin shook his head. "You two go on. I'll finish lunch with Sunny and Chav."

After we sat at the new table, a small one near the kitchen, I sipped my coffee and glared at Dominic.

He ordered an iced tea then turned to me and said, "What?"

In a quiet shout, the kind that's all about tone without

volume, I said, "What top secret information did you learn that Eldin couldn't hear?"

"Other than what's in the files, there's nothing new to learn."

"But the victim is definitely a therianthrope?"

"They're rabbit shifters."

"That explains the five kids and another on the way. Though, we have a woman in town, a deer shifter, who would give those rabbits a run for their money."

"You mean Ruth Thompson."

I assessed him again. "I get you spent a week here a couple years back, but damn, you really paid attention."

"Ruth is a friend of Chav's."

A knot formed in my throat. "Just how well did you get to know Chavvah Trimmel?"

"As well as any man could with a jealous werewolf breathing down his neck."

I snorted. "So not as well as you'd have liked."

Dom winked at me, and the knot in my throat tightened.

"Do any of the victims have ties to Peculiar? I really don't see how any investigation here is going to produce a lead."

"Actually, there is one thing that ties them all together." He leaned forward. "They were all at the Tri-State Council Jubilee here in two summers ago."

"When did you find this out?" Because if it was sooner than the past four hours I was going to be unhappy.

"I got the information when I was driving here from

Springfield. You know Wilhelmina Boden, your dad's new deputy?"

"Oh, yeah, the red-head engaged to Brady Corman."

Dom's eyes darkened. "That's her. She was head of security for the Tri-State Council before her move to Peculiar. She managed to get her hands on a complete list of all the people who attended the event. She gave your dad and me a copy."

"Did you find out if there are any more killings in this same vein prior to the last three?"

He shook his head. "Not yet." I noticed for the first time how tired he looked around the eyes.

"We should get to the interviews with the Blonde Bear owners and staff. Mr. Lieberman's life may depend on it. Though I don't know what we can learn here. Strangers stick out like sore thumbs. I think Blondina and Roger would have told my dad if anyone around here fit the bill."

"That's just it." Dom rubbed his chin. "I think it's someone who lives here."

I nodded, not wanting to agree, but there was no other explanation. "We need to start a list of people who could leave town without drawing suspicion."

"Agreed," Dom said. "And we need to do it in a way that doesn't alert the unsub."

In a town of less than two-thousand people, my partner was asking for a whole lot of impossible, but there were other things to consider with this criminal.

"This guy is smart. Organized. So, let's narrow it down by skilled employment or white-collar work." I planted my elbow on the table as another thought occurred to me.

"This killer is real ballsy. He takes his victims outside their homes and returns them. That takes a lot of confidence."

I felt a hand on my shoulder and turned to see Sunny Haddock staring down at me. Her eyes were glazed, and her very worried-looking best friend stood behind her.

"What is it?"

Chav shook her head. "I've never seen her like this."

With a blank stare in my direction, Sunny said in a monotone voice, "Duck when you see the yellow man. Step over the crack. Skipped stones on the lake. Beware the lying owl. Falling glass. Death." Her voice grew even more hollow. "Death strikes at twelve." She blinked, her pupils flexing to focus. "What in the world? That's weird."

I let out a noisy breath I'd been holding. "You're not kidding."

CHAPTER SIX

"*Y*ou can't honestly tell me you believe in psychics?" I scanned the meeting room at City Hall full of nodding heads starting with my dad and ending with the mayor and his sketchy wife. In between, Chavvah Trimmel and Doctor Billy Bob Smith watched me with a certain amount of amusement. The only person in the room who acted as if they might be even the tiniest bit on my side was Dominic.

My dad walked around the ten-foot by three-foot table separating us. He put his hands on my shoulders. "Look, kiddo. I didn't think it was possible either." He shrugged. "At first. But Sunny here has a gift, and once you see it in action, it's hard to deny."

"You sound like one of those nut-jobs they interview on the *Aliens in History* program, Dad. Jesus."

"I love that show," Sunny said brightly. She pointed to her husband. "Babe loves it too. Especially that Nina Pappadapolous."

"She does know how to stroll into a pyramid with authority."

Sunny smirked. "Yeah, it's the stroll that makes her so fascinating."

The mayor, un-mayorally, grabbed his wife into his arms and kissed her passionately.

Chavvah groaned. "Get a room you two." She snapped her gaze to the doctor whose eyes had suddenly turned predatorially on her. "Keep it in your pants, wolf. At least until the wedding."

I whistled loudly, and everyone went silent. "Can we discuss this whole psychic thing seriously for one moment?" My tone was terse, but I didn't know why. Therianthropic men were prone to these kinds of displays with their mates as the mood beset them. I, myself, had witnessed my father kiss my mom stupid more than a couple of hundred times during my childhood and since. My only explanation, at least the only one I could admit too, was that I was jealous I didn't have someone in my life lowering my I.Q.

Mayor Trimmel ended the kiss with Sunny. Her cheeks were red and her eyes glazed. For a second, I worried she was going to start yammering about the yellow man again. But then she smiled.

Nope. She wasn't going into a trance. Just happily dazed by love. The familiar twist of jealousy curled my stomach. "Look, Nicole. I don't need you to believe me. I'm not trying to pull a fast one on you or extort money. In other words, I've got no skin in this game. You can listen to whatever I said to you, or you can choose to ignore it. It doesn't matter to me either way."

Chavvah cleared her throat. "You said 'Death strikes at twelve', Sunny."

"Oh." She squinched her nose then shook her head. "Maybe you should listen to that part. It sounds pretty serious to me."

"You think?" my dad interjected. He turned his back on me, a maneuver he'd used my whole life when he wanted me to know he was "good and done" with whatever we were discussing, and addressed Sunny. "Do you remember anything about your vision?"

She sighed. "One minute I am happily eating my veggie burger and scarfing on steak fries, and the next minute I am standing at Nicole and Dom's table. I felt the usual light-headedness and tingling that happens when a vision is coming on, but it's never been like a sleep-walking thing. Usually, you know," she pointed at the carpet, "I end up on the floor. And," she added, "usually, I see the vision as if I'm living in it. Like it's real. But this was different. No walkthrough. It was more like a blur of pictures, and I didn't stay on any image long enough to get a clear look. I'll be damned if I can explain my ramblings. I don't remember saying any of those things."

"Just to be safe, I think I ought to assign a deputy to you, puddin."

"Da-ad," I whined. "Ix-nay on the uddin-pay."

Dominic raised a brow at me. "I'm fluent in Pig Latin." He leaned in conspiratorially. "F.Y.I. I can also spell, you

44

know, just in case you were planning that tactic in the *ef u tee u ar e*." His breath on my neck made me shiver.

"Got it." I shifted focus by blurting, "All the victims have a tie to Peculiar. They attended the Tri-State Council Jubilee when it was held here."

Chavvah groaned. "The gift that just keeps giving."

"How did you figure that out?"

"I have an, er, contact in the Council."

Sunny grinned. "You had Willy call the new security chief, didn't you?" She pointed at Dom. "Oh, yes, she told me all about your torrid little affair a few years back."

Jesus. Dom had dated Chavvah and Willy Boden. For a guy who wasn't from Peculiar, he sure got around. "We think the killer is from here."

"It has to be someone who travels for a job or leisure," Dom addressed my dad. "Is there any way to get a list of people who fit this profile?"

My dad's shoulders slumped. "Believe it or not, I don't know everyone in town. Not even some of the folk who have been here before I was born. There are less than two-thousand residents in town, but the more rural areas have probably a thousand or more. Some people only come to town when they need supplies. It won't be easy."

"What about you, Billy Bob?" Sunny asked. She turned her attention to Doctor Smith. "You treat almost every-body around here."

Doc's silver eyes narrowed to slits. "I can't divulge confidential patient information."

"Technically, we don't need a warrant to access your patient files," Dom said. "HIPAA rules afford law enforcement access when we are trying to identify a suspect. Besides that, the Tri-Council doesn't recognize the privacy of therianthropes during murder investigations. It boils down to this: This killer is drawing unwanted attention to a therianthropic community. We don't want humans to get more involved."

Doctor Smith nodded. "Only if there is cause. You don't have cause to look at all my patient records. I'm sorry, but none of my patients jump out as killers to me. If any of them did, I would tell you. And if you narrow it down to a couple of suspects, I'm happy to cooperate, but until then, I'm not going to let you go on a scavenger hunt through my files. I want to help but not like this. I'm not sure anyone in this room would want the police or any stranger going through their private medical matters. It's too invasive."

"I agree with Doc," Chavvah said. No surprise there. "What about that stupid city survey we had to fill out last year?"

"Oh!" Sunny nodded. "I know exactly the one you mean. It got pretty damn personal. At one point, I thought it was going to ask for my bra size. It had quite a few questions about employment, which is exactly what you all need. Maybe the mayor," she touched her husband's shoulder, "can ask Dovey Michaels, on the down-low mind you, if anyone has any jobs that require a lot of travel."

Mayor Trimmel put his arm over Sunny's shoulder, but he addressed the lot of us. "Dovey takes her job as the city's Budget and Management Director very seriously. I'm not sure she'll give me any private information about our citizens."

"I think we all know that Dovey has a sweet tooth for the boss." She slapped her husband on the butt. "Just smile and shake that ass, honey. That woman will give you anything you want."

Babel chuckled. "There's only one woman I want anything from."

"I find your devotion touching." Sunny put her hand on his chest and raised up on her toes to kiss his cheek. "Now, go flirt your way into Dovey's drawers." When Babel raised his brow, she added, "Her file drawers."

The young mayor laughed. "I guess I'll go sweet talk a bureaucrat."

Sunny elbowed him. "You're a bureaucrat. A bootie-licious bureaucrat, at that." She smacked him on the bottom for emphasis.

I interrupted their cutesy banter. "Maybe I should go talk to her. Dovey used to babysit me when I was little."

"You're still little," Dom muttered.

I flashed a smile that was all teeth and quietly said, "Dynamite comes in small packages."

"I bet the explosion is spectacular," he said in the same hushed manner.

Chavvah crossed her arms. "You do realize we're all shifters in this room, and we can hear you."

"Not all of us!" Sunny exclaimed. "What did I miss?"

I took a second to latch onto the one part of her exclamation that didn't put the focus on me. "What do you mean by not all of us?"

Her pert mouth formed an "O". She covered it with her hand. "Oops."

Dom cocked his head sideways at the mayor's wife. "Sunny is...Are you a human?"

"I like to think of myself as..." She threw up her arms. "Oh, who am I kidding? In a few years when I start looking my age, it's not like I'm going to be able to keep it a secret."

"You have got to be kidding me," I said. "This is a therianthropic community. No humans allowed. No humans are supposed to even know about us."

Dom put his hand on my shoulder. The warmth of his fingertips pressed into my skin. "You can't think that there are no humans who know about us. There are integrators all over the world who have mated cross-species. I just didn't expect to see it here in Peculiar."

I glared at my dad. "Me either." How had mom managed to keep it a secret? That woman couldn't keep her mouth shut about me starting my period when I was sixteen. How in the world had she kept quiet about this?

"I made her swear to silence," my dad said as if he could read my mind. "Your mom wanted to tell you, but we both agreed that this was too important for everyone to know about."

"So, the town doesn't know."

"Only the town council," he said. "The Johnsons, the Thompsons, the people in this room, and my deputies. We discussed it when she first moved to Peculiar and agreed to keep Sunny's secret, and that we would never speak of it in public or private. It was the only way to assure she could stay in town without interference from therians who would insist she leave, and also from the Tri-State Council, who, as you know, would investigate us to Hell and back if they found out."

I didn't know why the secret felt like a betrayal, but it did. I'd been gone from Peculiar for almost a decade, but this was the first time it hadn't felt like home.

"You can't tell anyone," Chavvah said.

She moved toward me, but Doc Smith put his hand out. "Nic won't tell a soul." His gaze darkened as it pivoted to Dominic. "How about you, Agent Tartan? Will you be reporting Sunny to the council?"

"Truthfully, I like Sunny, but I don't know. I am duty bound to the council even more than I am to the FBI. However, I won't do anything rash, and whatever I decide, I will give you all a heads up."

Babel Trimmel growled, his lip curling with anger. It was Sunny who stopped him by placing herself between her husband and my partner. "It's all right, Babe." He snarled but stayed put. She smiled at Dominic. "Right now, Dom has more to worry about than me." She walked over and took his hand. After a moment, she gave it a single, satisfied pat. "Dom will make the right decision."

The whole room seemed to sigh in relief. Except for Dom. His shoulders tensed and his jaw flexed. "Yes," he said tightly. "I will."

The door flung open to the room. Eldin Farraday stumbled in, sweaty and out of breath. "You are not...going to...believe...this," he said through labored pants. He held up the evidence baggy with the loyalty card. "We have partial matches on three prints other than the Messers."

"The FBI database came up clean," Dom said. "No matches."

"We have a local database," my dad said. "Eldin here is a computer whiz. He set it up a few years back so we could do local searches. Really, it's all we need."

Eldin, who'd finally caught his breath, nodded. "And you are not going to believe who the prints belong to, Sheriff."

My dad waved his hand at Eldin. "Go on, now. Don't bury the lead, son."

"Gary Davis, Mallory Evans, and Darrel Tolliver."

I cringed. The names told me exactly why Eldin was so excited. "God, I hate Hume's Day Preppers."

CHAPTER SEVEN

I had plans to meet Eldin for dinner at six-thirty. It would give me a chance to talk to the Messers about the preppers since we hadn't been able to talk to them at lunch. I shivered as I thought about the TSS. Those people were cah-razy from way back.

I jumped at the knock on my bedroom door. "Come in, Dominic."

The door opened. Dom led with his head, his dark mop of curls brushing his forehead. When his eyes pivoted up to meet mine, I sighed. Damn, the man was gorgeous with a capital G. "How'd you know it was me?"

"Maybe I'm a little psychic, too." I smirked when his eyes widened, and I shook my head. "I used my deductive skills. Mom would have just walked in, and my dad always announces himself when he knocks. Since you didn't barge in or announce yourself..."

"And I'm the only other person in the house..."

"Exactly. It doesn't take a mentalist to put it together."

"What is your take on the whole Sunny Trimmel thing?"

I shrugged and pulled my hair back, acutely aware of Dom's gaze on my neck. "I don't know. My dad has a good sense of people. If he trusts her, I'm inclined to do the same, but this whole psychic business... I don't know. It just sounds far-fetched."

Dom nodded. "Maybe. But let's keep an open mind for now." He pointed to my bed. "Can I sit?"

"Be my guest." I took a seat at my vanity and tried not to imagine what Dom would look like stretched across my pink comforter without clothes on.

He gave me an assessing look then smiled. "You're picturing me naked, aren't you?"

I blinked. "I am not." I mean, I had been trying really hard not to, anyhow.

His smile turned wolfish, which was really weird for a bear. "Tell me about these three people. These, what did you call them? Hume's day preppers?"

"They actually call themselves TSS, the Therianthrope Survival Society. Which is a real fancy name for a bunch of doomsday weirdos. They believe that when humans find out about therians, there will be a reckoning. The humans will come and exterminate us.

"In a way, it's sort of what we talked about this morning. People are scared of what they don't know. They are scared of anything different from themselves. The TSS believe that if it ever gets out that we exist, it will be an extinction level event for our kind." I shivered.

"It's an extreme point of view. Unfortunately, the

theory has enough teeth. I can see why some would believe it's true. How long has the group been around? And how many are there?"

"TSS has been around for about fifty years or thereabouts. I would say there are probably close to a hundred people at their compound. They own several patches of land near the lake. Dad has had a few run-ins with them. Mostly drunk and disorderlies." I chuckled. "They have their own stills and make a potent moonshine. Nothing dangerous though. These are the kind of folk who want to avoid drawing attention to themselves. I can't see them doing these abductions or the murders."

"We'll have to interview them."

I nodded. "They'll give some pushback. They are scared of humans, but they have a severe dislike of integrators. You and I are integrators. They see us as a threat to their existence. What if we pop a nail or grow fur at the wrong time around the wrong human? We might be better off letting my dad handle the TSS interviews, or at least bring him or Eldin along to soothe the path."

"These guys sound like a real stable bunch. I agree to having an escort, but not Farraday."

I'd been distracted thinking about the preppers, but Dom's dismissal of Eldin drew me back to the now. "Would you prefer Deputy Boden?"

It was Dom's turn to blink. "I...no, of course not," he sputtered.

"Eldin is a fully capable lawman, and he's worked longer for my dad than any of his other deputies. Besides, I trust him completely."

Dom's mouth thinned into a grim line. "Completely, huh."

I stood up and grabbed my purse from the floor. "I'm late for dinner. I'll report on what I learn from the Messers when I get back."

Before I could get past him, Dom reached out and snagged my wrist. Him sitting on the edge of the bed while I stood there put us at nearly the same height. His gray-green eyes were stormy as he stared at me. "Don't..." He let go of me and shook his head. "Don't treat the Messers like witnesses or suspects. Treat them like old friends."

"Yeah. I know. They're more likely to give information to me if they think it's social and not official." I tugged my arm from his loose grip.

Dom stood up. "I'll see you when you get back. Wake me if it's late, and we'll go over a plan for tomorrow."

My skin tingled where he'd grasped me. I resisted the urge to rub my wrist. I didn't want him to know how much he affected me. "Okay," I said more breathlessly than the situation warranted. "I'll see you when I get back."

I SHOVED A LARGE FRY in my mouth, and almost spit it out as it burned the crap out of my tongue. "Ow," I breathed around the hot as hell potato.

"You always do that," Eldin said. He took a bite of his burger. A rivulet of juice dripped down his chin.

After I managed to swallow the crispy coal, I laughed.

"And you always do that." I grabbed his napkin and tossed it at his chest. "Wipe your face, caveman."

His tongue snaked out of his mouth, and he licked at the beef juice, managing to smear it around and make an even bigger mess.

I giggled. He laughed. It took me back to being sixteen again. "You always could make me smile," I said.

"It's a gift." He grabbed the napkin and wiped his chin. His expression blanked then turned serious. "This used to be a quiet town."

"You mean during the decade that Neville Lutjen was selling out our kind to hunters?" I shook my head.

A lock of his brown hair fell over his green eyes. "When you put it like that it makes me sound naive."

"I think we all were. A bunch of ostriches with our heads in the sand." I bit into another fry, still hot, but not scorching, and enjoyed the way the salt coated my throat. I wiggled the bit still in my hands at Eldin. "The way this killer mutilates his victims before he kills them, we can't afford to think of Peculiar as a safe place. Not now. Especially since the latest victim hasn't shown up dead."

Eldin pursed his lips for a moment then met my gaze. "You think this Lieberman guy might still be alive."

I shrugged. "Maybe. I think it's a possibility. The abduction was messy. He put up a fight. I think he is a survivor. Someone our unsub didn't expect."

"You know my uncle lives out at the compound, right?"

"That's right. I forgot Uncle John was a prepper."

"And you know, they aren't completely wrong. Coming

out to the world is a scary prospect." Eldin's gaze drifted for a moment. "Speaking of coming out—"

"I heard you were back in town," a deep voice interrupted. I looked up to see a massive man with a full beard, broad shoulders, and a bit of belly paunch. His brown eyes were hard but not threatening.

"Brandon?" I stood up, and as in high school, he towered over me. He was even taller than Dominic. Damn, bears were big. I smiled and shook his hand. "Brandon Messer. It's so good to see you."

The wariness he'd been carrying eased. "It's good to see you, Nic. It's been a long time."

"About ten years," I said. "We both got out of here after high school and never looked back."

"Until this year," Brandon agreed. "I'm home for good now. I hear you're with the FBI."

"Yep, that's me. Got a badge and everything." I smiled.

"Hey, Eldin," Brandon said to my dinner date.

"Brandon," Eldin nodded. "Why don't you sit a spell with us? It'll be just like when we were kids."

Brandon's shoulder tensed. "I can't. I'm cooking tonight for ma. I need to get back to the kitchen. How's your food?"

"The burgers and fries are awesome," I said. "Best in all of Missouri."

Eldin leaned forward. "I can't believe I don't weigh four hundred pounds."

"It's that fox metabolism," I said. "You were always a bean pole."

"That's the God's honest truth." Brandon smiled,

finally, and he visibly relaxed. At that moment, I realized he was nervous. But why?

Blondina came out of the kitchen, her face pinched with anxiety. She made a beeline for our table. "How you all doing tonight?" she asked with a forced sweetness. I'd never seen her so apprehensive. What in the hell was going on? And what were the Messers so afraid of?

"Hey, Blondina. Doing good." I gave her an easy smile. "How are you?"

"Sid called and said you'd be coming in to talk to me, Brandon, Roger, and Selena about one of our punch cards. I don't know what we can tell you, but ask away."

My father had a big mouth. So much for keeping my interviews social. "Not at all," I said. "We think one of your diners might have witnessed a crime in Springfield. We found one of at the scene of a crime. A man was abducted from his home a couple of nights ago, so the whole thing is time sensitive. Truth is, I really don't believe anyone from our area is involved," I lied, "but I have to tick every box if you know what I mean."

Blondina nodded emphatically. "I'm happy to help, sugar. Ask me anything you'd like."

Brandon averted his eyes toward the door. I saw an almost imperceptible shake of his head before darting his gaze back to Eldin and me. I turned to see what had drawn his attention.

Mallory Evans, a tall, curvy blonde, had walked into the restaurant. She froze for a moment with a mild look of confusion, then turned around and put her hand on the door.

"Eldin," I said in a tone that put the deputy on high alert. I nodded toward the door. "Mallory."

The woman flung the door open and took off in a sprint.

"Shit!"

"What's going on?" Blondina asked.

I took two twenty-dollar bills out of my purse and put it on the table. "We have to go." Eldin was already up on his feet and yanking his jacket on.

By the time we got out the door, Mallory was nowhere to be seen. I balled my fists and slammed them into my thighs. "Damn it!"

"Why would she run? She can't know we found her prints," Eldin said.

"Brandon tipped her off. Whatever's going on, he's in it up to his neck."

"With torture and murder? That's a leap."

I pulled out my cell phone and dialed "Agent Pain in My Ass."

"Hello," he answered.

"This is Nicole," I said.

"I know. What's going on?"

"Mallory Evans showed up at Blonde Bear Cafe tonight."

"And?"

"And she saw Eldin and me and took off. We lost her." Saying it out loud felt humiliating. The first time I officially come up against and suspect, and she just slips away. "Damn it, Dom. I should have had her."

"It's okay, Nic. Your dad is working on a warrant to

serve on the TSS compound. I'll see if he can put a rush on it, and I'll pick you up in town. We'll find her."

"She knows we're after her." My heartbeat pulsed hard in my throat. "What if she warns the others? What if we've missed our chance?"

"There will be other chances."

"How can you know that?"

"Because there always is."

A few seconds of silence passed. I closed my eyes, listening to his breathing. "Okay," I finally said. "Call me when Dad gets the warrant."

"Where will you be?"

"I have to talk to a bear about a prepper."

AFTER TWENTY MINUTES of getting nowhere with a certain stubborn restaurant owner about where her son had run off to, I resorted to whining. "Blondina, you have to tell us where Brandon went."

The large, blonde woman crossed her arms and shook her head. "My son hasn't done anything wrong."

"He clearly gave Mallory Evans a warning when she entered the restaurant tonight," I said, unable to keep the incredulity or the annoyance from my tone.

Her husband, Roger, who was even taller and bigger than his wife, put his arm around her shoulder in comfort. "He took off out the back a few minutes ago."

Eldin nodded. "Thanks, Roger."

Blondina turned a venomous look at him. "How could you?"

"Listen, Honey Bear," he said soothingly. "I agree with you about our boy. He is no criminal. But that doesn't mean he's not foolish. We're not doing him any favors by hiding anything from the police."

I put my hand on Blondina's arm. "Look. I'm not going to railroad Brandon. If he's done nothing wrong, I swear he'll get a fair shake. You know my dad isn't going to let anyone innocent go down for something he didn't do."

"But it's not just local police involved, is it?" Blondina gave me the stink eye. "I trust Sheriff Taylor. I don't trust the FBI."

I nodded. "Don't trust the FBI then." I squeezed her arm. "Trust me. I promise to be diligent and fair. Now, do you know where Brandon might go?"

"First, tell me what this is about? I'm not giving you any information until I know why you're here, Nic."

"It's an ongoing investigation, Blondina," Eldin said. "We're not allowed to share any information."

I cast him a grateful glance. In the periphery, I saw my dad, Dom, and a man I recognized as Judge Harrison Holt. He'd been the judge for the Peculiar Municipal Court for twenty years. I hoped his presence meant they were able to get the warrant.

Blondina, a strong and proud woman, teared up when she saw my dad. "Oh, Sid." She clutched her chest. "You know my boy. He isn't a criminal."

My dad walked right up to her and put his hand on her

shoulder. "No one is saying he is." He looked at Roger. "How does Brandon know Mallory Evans?"

The female bear shifter shook her head emphatically. "I don't know. That's the honest truth. His divorce was official last month. I don't think he'd be dating again so soon. That Samantha broke his heart. It's why he moved back home."

Judge Holt spoke up, his brown eyes sharp with intelligence. "I've signed the warrant to search the TSS compound, but Sheriff Taylor, I think I should go out there with you all."

"Why?" Dom asked and earned an irritated glance.

My dad said, "Judge Holt grew up on TSS land, his father was one of the founders."

"Now, I don't ken with all that they believe. It's why I went off to college as soon as I graduated high school and earned a law degree. I believe that if the humans ever find out about us, we're going to need people who know the law." He looked at Dom and me. "Like you two. You do a great service for our people."

"Thank you," I said. "Do you still have ties out on the compound?"

"I have some cousins and an uncle. My dad died years ago. Since he's been gone, I don't have much reason to visit, but I still go to occasional social gatherings. It's the reason I want to go when you serve the warrant. My kinfolk and the other families are heavily armed, and I don't want any of them to be punished because of paranoia. While I find it hard to believe any of the three people on the warrant are involved in this crime, the fingerprints on the card are enough evidence, as far as I'm concerned, to question them."

Dom's brow furrowed, making him look downright grumpy. "It's acceptable to us. Let's go."

My dad circled his finger in the air. "I'll call Deputy Thompson to meet us at the compound gates with tactical gear."

The judge pinched the bridge of his nose. "Is that necessary? I really don't believe this is going to come down to a firefight."

"Maybe. Maybe not," my dad responded. "But I'm not going to take a chance with my people."

I knew he mostly meant me, his daughter, but hey, I didn't disagree. "We have a couple of vests in the trunk of our vehicle."

"Good." My dad turned on his heel toward the front door. "Let's go."

CHAPTER EIGHT

*T*he perimeter of the compound featured high, rough stone walls and a wrought iron gate with motion sensor video cameras. We parked far enough back from the activation area and waited for Tyler Thompson to arrive with the gear. The cold February chill turned even more miserable as Mother Nature added rain to mix.

"This is going to suck," Dominic said as I turned the engine off.

"We could always wait for the spring," I replied.

"Smart ass." He smelled like lime and verbena. I congratulated myself for not leaning over and taking a big whiff.

"Yep." I caught sight of headlights in my rearview mirror and breathed a sigh of relief. I needed a distraction from Dom's invigorating scent. If I was honest, I was *this close* to licking the man. A second later, the lights went out as the vehicle drew closer to us. It was a sheriff's car. Deputy Thompson had arrived. As the young deputy got out, people exited my dad's truck. I put my hand on the door latch. "Go time."

Exiting the car felt like stepping into a margarita—with the blender on full spin. Dad gave me and Dom black plastic ponchos from the back seat of his truck.

"Always prepared," I said.

"Can't take the credit. Your mother put them in there. She loves the weather channel."

In a way, I guess Mom was a prepper. I smiled. "I'm glad to have it." I tucked my hands inside. My fingertips tingled as I wiped the dampness onto my shirt.

"You okay?" Dom asked.

"Yes. Raccoon therians have sensitive receptors in their hands and feet that allows us to identify objects and items by touch alone."

"That sounds handy."

"Ha ha." I rolled my eyes. "Getting my hands wet makes them uber-sensitive. Unbearably so."

Dad nodded. "It only get's worse as we get older." He absently rubbed his fingertips together.

"So, you all are good with your hands." Dom smirked. "I'll file that away as information I didn't know." He rubbed his arms. "It's freezing out here."

"It's not so bad. If it wasn't raining, it would be comfortable enough."

"What? Raccoons don't get cold?"

I smirked. "Yeah, sure. But it takes colder temperatures than what we've been experiencing. Besides, I thought bears ran hot."

"We do. Which is why we're affected by the cold. I'd go

and hibernate right now if someone offered me a warm cave."

I could tell by his amused look he was kidding. Besides, I'd grown up with bear shifters, and none of them ever hibernated during the winter.

Eldin joined Dom and me. "Ready to go?"

I nodded. "I am itching to get in there."

Deputy Thompson sidled up next to us. "I've never been to the compound before. This should be interesting."

He pulled a mustard-colored rain poncho out of its pouch and put it on. A boom of thunder made me jump right before a loud pop sounded, and my car window shattered. I threw myself on the muddy gravel road, rocks biting into my knees.

"What the hell!" Dom shouted as he hit the ground next to me along with Thompson and Eldin. I looked for my dad, and he and the judge had already crawled behind his truck. He waved at me to move for cover, but it wasn't necessary. Dom had already grabbed me and was dragging me toward the ditch. I gained my feet and crouch-ran the rest of the distance on my own. The two deputies scrambled for cover as well.

"Jesus." Dom frantically patted me down, my arms, my shoulders, neck, and face. "Are you okay?"

"Fine, fine." I put my hands over his. "The bullet missed me."

A loud voice came over a megaphone. "This is Judge Harold Holt. I'm with Sheriff Taylor and other law enforcement to serve a warrant. Put your weapon down. Open the gate and clear the way."

"Is that you, Harry?" a man shouted. "Sorry. Sorry. No one's hurt, are they?"

"We're fine, Cal. Now put the weapon down and come out here."

The metal gate hummed as it slowly opened. The silhouette of a man stood in the opening. He had his hands raised high. "I'm sorry. I thought you all were trespassers. We've been getting some weirdos out here lately."

"That's a bit of the pot calling the kettle black," I whispered to Dom.

"Anyhow," Cal continued as he stepped closer. "The thunder startled me, and I accidentally squeezed the trigger on my rifle."

Cal was Calvin Riggs, a long time TSS member. I'd seen him in town over the years but didn't know much about him other than what he looked like. I stood up and glanced over at Deputy Thompson, his yellow poncho streaked with mud, and shook my head.

Duck when you see the yellow man. Was this Sunny Trimmel's prediction fulfilled, or was it a coincidence? My mind leaned toward coincidence, but my gut told me I should watch the ground for cracks.

My dad and the judge were talking to Cal, who was doing a lot of nodding, gesticulating, and looking contrite.

"We should go introduce ourselves," Dom said. He balled his fist as anger rolled off him like steam off a warm pond in the snow. "This is our investigation, and that idiot is going to spend the night in jail tonight for attempted assault on an FBI agent."

I held my hand out to stop him. "I want to get in there

as bad as you do." Because Cal had earned a punch in the mouth from me. "The guy's a total dumbass, but we'll get further with these bozos if we let Dad do his thing. They won't trust you or me."

I noticed his fists were shaking with barely contained rage as the muscle in his jaw rapidly flexed. "He could have killed you."

I calmed my own anger with a deep breath. I let it out slowly and said, "But he didn't." I touched Dom's face to direct his gaze off of Cal Riggs and onto me. "I'm fine."

Dom's stormy expression didn't waver. "When this is over, him and I are going to have a talk."

"Agreed. But right now, he isn't our priority. We have three suspects to round up, and we can't afford to divide our attention." I smiled. "Besides. My dad's jail only has two cells. There isn't enough room to round up everyone you're going to get pissed at before the night is over."

"Is that your professional opinion?" His hands had stopped shaking. Good.

"Indeed."

"Nic. Agent Tartan," my dad shouted. He waved us over. "We're clear to go in."

"We're up, puddin'."

I glared at Dominic. "Shut up." While I acted aggravated, really, I was relieved he'd relaxed enough to tease me.

We followed Cal into the compound, and I'm ashamed how fascinated I was with the place. It would have made a great research project for my undergrad degree. The psychological issues associated with walling yourself off from everyone and everything beyond your small community was rooted in deep paranoia. The rain had turned into a bearable but unpleasant mist. My stylish boots were scraped and muddy, and my pants were ruined—although Mom had been known to work laundry miracles.

I counted at least a dozen bright-white buildings. Even though my raccoon vision was excellent, I didn't need it to view the structures. A flash in the sky revealed a large water tower off to the right. I shielded my eyes as large stadium-like lights turned on around the compound. Two men stood in an open doorway of the first building. The welcome wagon, if I had to guess.

As we drew closer, the two men went inside, and we all trailed in after them. There was no floormat to wipe our feet on, but the muddy and wet tracks on the smooth, gray concrete indicated the TSS didn't care whether we mucked up their floors. Twelve folding, metal picnic tables filled the interior space. On the far end of the wall was a table that held one of those silver, 30-cup percolator coffee pots and a stack of foam coffee cups. To the right of the door was a counter, and beyond the opening, I could see a stove and a refrigerator. A community kitchen, maybe?

The place reminded me of an AA meeting I attended once with a friend my junior year of my undergrad. It had been held in V.F.W. building with a similar setup. It made me wonder if some of the TSS might have a military background. I made a note to ask my dad if he could do background checks on some of the old-timers. Or maybe the judge would know. He'd grown up here, after all.

The two men—one short and thin, with dark hair and

eyes, the other medium height, with an average build. The average man's only stand out feature was his almost color-less blue eyes that contrasted heavily with his black hair. His eyes reminded me of opossum shifters, but they tended to have white hair as well.

He took off his jacket, and there was a lanyard holding eyeglasses around his neck. It confirmed my hunch. Opossums had a great sense of smell, but lousy eyesight. They were one of the few therians I knew whoever had to wear glasses.

"Have a seat," the man said. "I'm Andy Lark, and this is Lloyd Evans."

The small guy had the same last name as Mallory. Wow. The family tree must've been split somewhere because she was much larger. "Are you and Mallory Evans related?"

All eyes shifted in my direction.

Dom cleared his throat. "Please answer the question."

He looked at my dad and the judge. The judge nodded.

Evans glared at me. "She's my cousin. The daughter of my Uncle Tibor." He took a small plastic container from the breast pocket of his T-shirt, pulled out a thin, white toothpick and stuck it in his mouth. He worried it between his teeth with intensity.

The judge sat down at the table. "How is Ti? He had a bum knee the last time I saw him."

"It's better, Judge. I'll tell him you asked." Evans gnawed the plastic toothpick with more intensity.

"How long has it been?" I asked.

He frowned at me. "I don't know what you're talking about."

"Since your last cigarette," I said.

"About five minutes past mind your own fucking business," the small man quipped.

Before I could respond, the judge rapped his knuckles on the table. "Why don't we all sit down so we can discuss the current situation?"

My dad stayed on his feet. He passed the warrant across the table to Lark. "We have a warrant for the arrest of Mallory Evans, Gary Davis, and Darrel Tolliver. You can either encourage them to come in with us of their own volition, or we can search every building on your compound."

"Our home," Lark insisted. "We're not a cult."

"This isn't exactly the suburbs," I noted.

He bared his teeth at me. "We are a gated community."

"I'm betting the homeowner dues are ridiculous."

Before I could say more, Dom intervened. "Will those three turn themselves over for questioning or do we need to start tearing this place apart?"

"Now, just hold on there," the judge said. "No one is going to tear anything apart. We don't want any trouble."

"Why do you want them for?" Evans asked. "Mallory has never been in trouble a day of her life, and Gary and Darrell are as law-abiding as the day as long."

My dad spoke up this time. "There is evidence that suggests one or all of them at the scene of a crime in Springfield. We're not at liberty to discuss more with you."

"I don't like it, Harry," Lark said. His pale eyes narrowed to slits. "Who is this guy?" He indicated Dom.

"Relax, now," said Dad. "He's a bear shifter."

"I'm Special Agent Dominic Tartan with the Federal Bureau of Investigation."

"You have got to be kidding me," Lark said incredulously. "A damned integrator?"

"Dom's also an investigator for the Tri-Council,"added Judge Holt.

"We only recognize our own authority here," said Lark. "You know that, Harry."

"Believe what you want," said the judge. "But you know as well as I do that the TSS is under the auspices of the Tri-Council."

Lark's expression blackened. He turned a hateful gaze onto Dom but kept his silence.

Evans apparently had less sense than his friend. He kicked under the table at the open chair near my dad and sent it sliding across the concrete. "How could you bring an integrator into our community, Harry?"

"There is nothing I can do about it, Lloyd, even if I wanted to. The law's the law."

Evans glared at Dom. "Human lover."

I looked at Dom with a shocked expression. "Is that true, partner? Are you a human lover?" I shook my head. "Say it ain't so."

"I love everyone," Dom said seriously.

Evans stood up. "This is bull shit."

Dom reached across the table quicker than I thought possible for a man his size and grabbed Evans by the front of his shirt. Dom put his face near the now sputtering man's and growled. "Except this guy." He shook his head. "I don't love this guy." Evans' eyes bugged as Dom let him go and settled back into his own seat.

Deputy Thompson and Eldin, who had both hung back, were now moving toward the table, their hands on their weapons. Dad held up his hand. "Mister Evans, I'd hate to haul you in tonight as well, considering there is only enough room in Deputy Thompson's backseat for three prisoners." He pulled the chair back to the table and put his foot upon it for effect. "Of course, I've always liked hood ornaments. Would you like to be my hood ornament?"

This time, Evans was smart enough to keep his mouth shut.

Judge Holt nodded his approval. "If Mallory, Gary, and Darrell have alibis for the time of the crime, we can rule them out. They are not doing themselves any favors by hiding."

"Fair enough," said Lark. He glanced at Evans. "Go get them."

A few minutes later, the three suspects were delivered to us. Eldin and Tyler handcuffed them and read them their rights before we all returned to our cars.

When I was back in the driver seat, I looked at Dom. "Didn't that seem a little too easy?"

He shrugged. "I've seen it go down that way before. Sometimes, it is what it is."

"Maybe." I tapped my chin.

"What are you thinking?"

"I think that the preppers are people who don't give up their freedom for any reason. It goes against the whole doomsday philosophy they live by. I just think it's strange that Lark and Evans turned them over without a fight."

"Do you think Brandon Messer is at the compound?" He shook his head. "Whoops, I mean gated community." He finger-quoted the final two words. "Seriously. Who does that jackass think he's fooling with that crap?"

"Probably nobody. It seemed more rote propaganda than anything he actually felt strongly about. I'd say it was part of their recruitment speech." I mimicked Andy Lark. "Join our gated community and live out your days safely behind stone walls topped with razor wire as the rest of our kinds burns at the hands of humans." I glanced at a wide-eyed Dom. "Or something to that effect."

"They are nuts."

"Well, I think there's a couple of squirrel shifters in there." I looked at the time on car's rearview mirror. It was already ten o'clock. It was going to be a long night if we planned to talk to all three of them. "This day is never gonna end."

"Your dad's guys will get initial statements and try to collaborate alibis. No sense in talking to them yet. Let them cool in jail overnight. A stint behind bars might make one of them break."

I snorted. "My dad's jail is like staying at a motel. Not an upscale one, mind you, but it's not going to scare anyone straight if that's what you think."

"Still," Dom said. "We've been on the road since nine this morning. I think we should sleep on this. Have our minds fresh for tomorrow."

Reluctantly, I nodded as a yawn escaped me. "I really am tired."

"Then as the senior agent of this team, I'm going to insist."

"Fine," I said, starting the car. "I'd hate to be insubordinate on my first day."

Dom snorted. "Too late for that."

CHAPTER NINE

I stretched, inhaling the sweet scent of raspberries. I gathered my covers to my face and embraced the feeling of home. The shower turned on in the bathroom next to my room, and I heard a baritone voice singing Neil Diamond's "Sweet Caroline."

My throat felt thick and dry as I imagined hot, soapy suds sheeting down Dominic's back and over his muscular butt. I crossed my legs as my lower bits began to ache. All kinds of diabolical plans for "accidentally" opening up the bathroom door as he stepped out of the shower played out in my head. There wasn't a single one that wasn't a cliché, but my throbby parts just didn't care. I bit back a groan as the singing stopped after two verses and several rounds of the chorus.

"I will not drool over my partner," I whispered. "I will not drool over my senior partner." I wiped at the small amount of spittle that wet the corner of my mouth. "I

stand corrected. I, apparently, will drool over my partner."
Ugh. I hated myself.

A soft knock at the door froze me in place.

It came again, along with Dom's voice. "You up?"

"Yes," I squeaked then normalized my voice, and
repeated, "Yes. I'm up. I'll be down in a minute."

"Okay," he said. "Meet you downstairs for coffee. I
think your mom made blueberry and currant scones."

"Sounds good." I was still full from pigging out on carbs
the night before, but there was always room in my tummy
for scones. Nothing like breakfast pastries to get my mind
off of sex. "Gah!"

"Are you okay?"

"Shit." He was still at the door. "I'm fine. Go. I'll be
down in a few." I threw the covers over my head then
threw them back and slung my legs over the side of the
bed. Hello, day. Time to adult.

I'd showered the night before, so all I really had to do
was wet my hair a little, pull it back, brush my teeth, get
some mascara on, and a little concealer around my eyes. It
took thirteen minutes from bed to breakfast. And, oh my
gosh, mom's scones were woke!

Dominic took a sip of coffee from a mug that said, *You
have the right to remain silent... at least until I've had my first cup
of coffee.* He twirled his index finger at me. "Agent Taylor,
you're peppering your pants with crumbs."

"Snacks for later," I told him and shoved the last bite of
my current scone in my mouth. I washed it down with the
chai latte mom had made special for me with her new one-
cup brewer. She glanced at me from the sink where she

was doing up a few dishes. "This is awesome, Mom. All of it."

"Since I forced you to stay here, the least I can do is make it hospitable."

"More than," Dominic praised. "I haven't been treated this well in, well, ever."

"You mean there's not a woman somewhere waiting to take care of you, Agent Tartan?"

I snorted chai out my nose and started coughing as a result. Mom gave me a worried glance. "You okay, Puddin'?"

My eyes bulged at the nickname, but I couldn't complain because I was still choking on the hot liquid. Dom walked around the center island and proceeded to slap me on the back. Mom tried to make me drink water as if more liquids would help. Finally, I wheezed in a breath. "Enough!" I slid off the stool and took a few steps away from both of my hapless saviors.

I dusted my pants off. "We need to get down to the jail." I wiped the choke tears from my eyes, grateful my mascara was waterproof, or I'd have resembled my animal side. I got called bandit once in school after a band event in the rain and my mascara blackened my eyes. After blaming my mother, like a teenager will do, I learned not to make that mistake again. When I could see again, I grabbed a paper towel to get the snorted chai off my face.

"You okay," Dom asked.

I nodded, but couldn't look at Dom. I was too embarrassed, so I kept my head down and tried not let it show. "Let's go. Time's a' wasting."

"Nicole's right, Mrs. Taylor," Dominic said to my disappointed mother. "But to answer your question. No, there is no one waiting to take care of me at home." I didn't want to feel pleased by his relationship status, but I was. Damn it. Dominic bent down and gave my mom a quick peck on the cheek. "And please, call me Dom."

"Thank you, Dom. You can call me Mrs. Taylor." She winked at him. "For now, anyhow. And for future reference, the guest bathroom downstairs has a working shower."

Dominic blanched.

I almost choked again, this time on laughter. Had he really showered in my bathroom to get my attention? He'd underestimated my ability to resist peeking at him naked. Hah! I guess I showed him. I didn't even get out of bed. Nope. I just hid under the covers like the mature, young woman I am.

"You got it, Mrs. Taylor."

When we got to the car, Dom paused behind the open passenger door. "Your mom is one cool customer."

God love the woman, she knew how to unsettle people when it suited her. "She certainly is, partner. And observant. Believe me, I get away with nothing around her, and neither does anyone else."

"I will keep that in mind."

On the way into town, I couldn't get the TSS out of my head. "There's something fishy going on with those preppers."

"All the victims have been integrators. Maybe the TSS has decided to start taking out shifters that they think are human lovers."

I shook my head. "So far, the murders have the hall-marks of one killer. The MO is the same—especially with the taking the pinky toes as souvenirs. A group effort wouldn't be that clean. If they wanted to take out integrators, why not a more concerted effort with more victims?"

"Okay. One person. There have been three murders that we know about, so we're talking serial killer."

"Worse. We're talking about a shifter serial killer. We don't have any statistical information about shifters with Antisocial Personality Disorder. I'd like to think it's because APD is rare with our kind."

"But?"

"It might be because shifters are dual-natured. Who we are in our animal forms is very different from who we are as humans."

"More primal, you mean."

"Exactly. I'd like to think that I am analytical and careful, but sometimes my animal nature gets the better of me. I spend a lot of time hiding my impulses. I'm sure it's the same for you."

"It can be difficult at times. Especially living amongst humans."

"Exactly. Which means, it might be easier for a shifter to hide a personality disorder." I'd always found the way people behaved fascinating. And shifters, doubly so. It was one of the reasons I wanted to be a profiler. "Did you know that one percent of the population in the United States are violent psychopaths? And that one percent is estimated to be the cause of fifty-percent of all violent crimes?"

"Actually, I did know that. You might not remember, but I'm an FBI agent."

"Yeah? Did you know that there are an estimated two million psychopaths in the US alone?"

Dom looked at me. "How does that square with one percent?"

I smiled. "Not all psychopaths are criminals. They're CEOs, doctors, lawyers, and other types of occupations that give them power over others."

"You're not giving me a lot of hope that we're gonna catch our guy—or girl."

"The ratio of male to female psychopaths is twenty to one. It's more likely we're dealing with a guy."

"Ah. But those are human statistics."

I nodded. "True." He had a point. I knew a few girls in school that I would have put in the category.

"So, our psycho is either goal-seeking or thrill-seeking."

"Very good, Special Agent Tartan. I'm leaning toward mission-oriented."

"Right. The killer thinks he is ridding his world of those he or she," he put the emphasis on she, "believes shouldn't breathe the same air as everyone else. I get it. And the TSS hates humans. But the dead guys aren't human."

"No," I said. "You're right. They aren't human. But they were all at the Jubilee. And they were all in Peculiar nineteen months ago."

"And they were all integrators," mused Dom. "That feels like the most important element to me."

We were only a couple blocks from the Sheriff's Station

when another thought popped into my head and burst my bubble. "Damn it."

"What?"

"Torture, mutilation. Those are not traits of a mission-oriented killer. These things fall under hedonistic thrill-seeker."

"A psycho is a psycho," Dom said as I parked in the Sheriff's parking lot next to a police car.

"Not really," I said. "If you want a viable profile, we need to go over the evidence again and determine which is more accurate."

Inside the station, Michael Connelly, a squirrel shifter and deputy, stood near my dad's office door. He was doing a lot of nodding. Over at a desk, a woman with a wild mane of red hair, typed away at a computer. Willy Boden. Dominic's ex-girlfriend. I'd met Willy back when my aunt was killed. She used solid investigating to track down my aunt's killer, so I knew she was smart and good at her job. She was also beautiful, but I wouldn't hold it against her.

"Hey, Deputy Boden," I said as we entered the room. "Nice to see you."

She swiveled in her chair and stood up, leading with her enormously protruding belly. Christ, was she having twins?

"Nicole Taylor, don't you look smart." Willy smiled as she waddled toward Dom and me. "Or it could be that everyone looks bright next to a dim bulb."

I chuckled when Dominic groaned.

"I'd ask how you're doing," Dom said. He pointed to her stomach. "But all the evidence points to pregnant with a chance of twins. Did you finally get over your commitment phobia, or is this one of those do-it-yourself projects?"

"Aren't you sweet to ask," she replied. "I'm banging the local handyman. He knocked me up so I couldn't get away from him."

"That's not exactly true," a man said behind us. He walked over to Willy and escorted her back to her chair. He was carrying a bag. "Sunny sent me with some poppy seed lemon muffins for you." He looked at a steaming mug on her desk. "That better be decaf."

"It's ginger tea for fucksake!" Willy plopped down grumpily. "I'm not a baby."

"No, but you're having one. Doc said you should be at home with your feet up. You want to work. So that means you have to put up with me worrying and doting."

I cleared my throat. "Hi, Mr. Corman."

Brady Corman had a long history in Peculiar. He had been the mayor fifteen or so years ago until his wife went missing. She'd been a victim of an opportunistic asshole who sold out our kind to hunters for profit. The worst kind of low-life. Mr. Corman had a small son to raise, but with his wife gone, he'd fallen apart. My mom and dad had always liked the Corman family, and it was nice to see the man happy again.

"Oh." He looked at me as if he'd just noticed there were more people in the room than he and Willy. "Nicole Taylor." He smiled. "What are you doing back in town?"

"Official business," I said.

He looked confused.

"F.B.I.," I added.

"Oh." He didn't look any less confused. He turned his head over his left shoulder and shouted. "Sid, Willy can be here for four hours. No more. Doctor's orders."

"Heard," my dad shouted back. "Willy, if you don't clock out at eleven and go home you will not be welcome back to work until those babies are out."

Willy sighed unhappily. "Heard," she muttered.

Brady Corman smiled. "Good. Now keep off your feet. Put them up when you can. I'll see you at home this afternoon."

"Don't you have a job?" Willy asked.

"Yes," he told her. He kissed her on the forehead. "Taking care of you."

Watching the exchange between the two of them, I was still jealous, but for different reasons. The two of them were awesome together. I wanted that in my own life.

I nudged Dominic. "Let's have Connelly bring Mallory in for our first interview."

He nodded, looking a little bewildered and a lot less tense. "I'm ready."

CHAPTER TEN

I handed Dom a note with questions I'd written down. The notebook paper felt rough on my fingertips. I had to admit I felt a little nervous. After all, he was the senior agent, and I was a newbie. But I also had good instincts about people—and shifters. A trait I no doubt owed to my parents who were both expert interrogators in their own way. Especially when quizzing their daughter about why she was late for curfew. Ahem.

Dom read the list, and then looked at me. "You know this isn't my first interrogation, right?"

"But it is mine." I tapped the back of the paper. "People, in general, don't like to lie. There is always the fear of getting caught, and so when they can avoid it, they will."

"Interrogation 101," said Dom. He reread the questions and nodded. "You want to know if she's a psychopath."

"Exactly. Psychopaths have no qualms about lying. For them, lying is the same as telling the truth. That's why lie detectors are ineffective. They test for fear not for dishonesty."

"Agents can be trained to pass lie detector tests. It doesn't mean they're psychopaths. And some people are just really good at lying even if they're not suffering from a personality disorder," said Dom.

"Mallory Evans is not a trained agent."

"How do you know? Seems to me the TSS trains their members to do a lot of things. They're all about preparing for the so-called war with humans."

Shit. I hadn't thought about that. Despite my education and my eagerness to do well, I was still inexperienced when it came to actual field work. That chafed at my ego. Patience had never been my strong suit. "Dom, these questions are meant to make Mallory nervous, force her to come clean, albeit reluctantly, or tell a white lie."

"In which case, she's not a psychopath."

"Or a trained TSS goon."

He smiled. My stomach dipped at that sensual curve of his lips. The man was too good-looking for his own damned good.

"Okay, Doc. We'll try it your way."

God, I loved a man who wanted to do things my way. "Thanks."

"I'll ask the questions—and you watch her physical reactions."

"Will do."

Dom tucked the list of questions into the folder he held. Then we walked into the interrogation room no bigger than a broom closet. Mallory Evans sat there with red, puffy eyes, her nails bitten down to the quick, and her hair looking like she'd twirled on her head all night. Her hands shook as she fumbled for the bottle of water Connelly had provided for her. Well, hell. She was either the most ingenious psycho ever or terrified. I opted for terrified.

"Mallory, why did you run away when you saw me last night?" I asked.

The curvy brunette sniffed, her dark eyes hardening as she met mine. She remained silent, but I could see the fear in her gaze. She was in full-on bluffing mode.

Dom glared at me, but he was too much of a professional to ream me outright. Yikes. Okay, I'd earned his ire. I'd flipped the script on him without notice, but I wasn't sorry I followed my instincts. Mallory was on teetering on the edge. I believed we could push her over.

"Innocent people don't run," Dom said.

This wasn't true. Innocent people went on the run all the time because they were scared of being presumed guilty. However, Dom wasn't trying to determine her innocence. He was using a classic interview technique. Most people didn't know that law enforcement officers had carte blanche to lie when conducting interrogations. Both human and shifter investigators rely on it as a tool used to rattle the person of interest. Innocent people got pissed-off. Guilty people usually back-pedaled or tried a different story than the one they'd told before.

"I want a lawyer," said Mallory.

"I want a million dollars," said Dom, taking the seat

across from Mallory. "Looks like we're both going to be disappointed."

I leaned against the wall, my arms crossed. Mallory's gaze darted around the small, dark room. Sweat dotted her brow and rolled down her temples. Her fear was tangible, so much so that I could smell—even taste its acridness.

"I know my rights. I'm entitled to a lawyer."

"For someone who's supposedly anti-human, you sure are eager to use their laws." Dom slapped the file onto the square metal table. Mallory's eyes were drawn to the manila folder. "We're in therianthrope territory, Ms. Evans. We follow shifter law. And that means you don't get a lawyer. You don't get released. You don't get a damned thing—unless I say so."

"Guilty until proven innocent," I chimed in. "That's the way it is for us. And you know it." Unfortunately for Mallory, we served up justice differently than the humans. If a therianthrope received a life sentence of one-hundred years or more, or hell, even forty years, humans would notice the slow aging and our secrets would be exposed. A century ago, shifters found guilty of heinous crimes were killed. At least these days, we attempted reform before ending their lives.

"I won't talk to no damn integrators," she spat.

"Brandon Messer was an integrator," I said casually. "You seem to be dealing with him all right."

The woman blanched. "He...he's not. He made a mistake, and he knows now. Knows it isn't right."

"So, he's a convert then? Did you personally convert him?"

"You think it's funny. You think I'm crazy. That we're all crazy. But, when the humans come for us, and they will, you will beg us for shelter."

"Therians have been worried about exposure since the dawn of man. It hasn't happened yet."

"In this day and age of technology, how long do you think it's going to be before the humans discover us? The end is coming! If you can't see that what I'm saying is true, then you've been living your lie among the humans for too long. You think they're your friends. They're not. They don't know you, and if they did, they would hate and fear you." Her speech was typical TSS rhetoric. I wondered how much of her diatribe was rote—and how much she actually believed.

I'll admit, her speech made my stomach hurt. She wasn't wrong about the humans never being able to know me. I had a couple of human boyfriends in college, and I hated constantly having to hide my true self from them, but they were nice guys, and I had two best friends that I trusted with every secret, except the biggest. I often wondered how they would have reacted to the truth. Would they have been accepting of me or terrified of the stranger they'd shared their own secrets with?

"Are you done?" asked Dom in a bored voice.

"You should be praising the efforts of the TSS. We are the last hope for our species."

"If that's the case, we're screwed." Dom opened the file and pulled out pictures of the three victims.

"What are those?"

He pushed the photos across the table. Mallory looked

down at them and blanched. "That's sick." She looked at Dom, her expression both appalled and furious. "You're sick."

"You just told us how much you hate humans. And you don't have much respect for integrators."

Mallory swallowed hard. "I haven't killed anyone."

"Hey, Agent Taylor, you like the Blonde Bear Café?" Dom's stern tone smoothed out.

"Best burger in town," I said.

"What about you, Ms. Evans?" Dom put the pictures back into the folder. "You a fan of the Blonde Bear Café?"

The switch from the accusatory tone and aggressive questioning to pleasant conversation and seemingly inane queries stunned Mallory into confused silence. I knew immediately where Dom was going with this new tactic.

"Probably not," I said. "The other night, she turned around and left as soon as she got in the door."

"Is that the real reason you left the café?" asked Dom. "You don't like their food?"

Mallory's gaze shifted from Dom to me and then back again. "It's all right, I guess."

"How much do you like the food there, Agent Taylor?"

"A lot. I even have one of those loyalty cards. Every time I eat at the café, the card gets punched. I'm two meals away from a free entrée."

"You got one of those cards, Mallory?"

"No," she said cautiously.

"You sure? Maybe you've used a friend's loyalty card."

Recognition flashed in her eyes. *Aha*, I thought, *we gotcha*.

"What are y'all going on about?" she asked.

Dom withdrew another photo—this one a close-up of the punch card. The fingerprint dust on the laminate showed five clear prints. "See these two prints on the left side?"

"Yeah. So?"

"They're yours." Dom's smile was feral. "This card was found at the scene of a crime. And I think you were there."

Mallory emitted a loud and obnoxious laugh. "That's what this is all about? The entire compound has touched that card, you idiots. We all take it with us when we go to town to get leadership dinners for Wednesday meetings or when someone is going into town for a meal. You guys are fucking geniuses."

"So you admit that this card can only be accessed by your TSS compatriots?" asked Dom.

Mallory lost her smile. She'd unwittingly implicated someone in the TSS by IDing the card as belonging to the group. "Well, now, I don't know," she said.

"If it doesn't belong to you or one of your friends, then the only explanation for your fingerprints on this card is that it belongs to the TSS." Dom tucked the picture away. "Unless you've been lying to me, Ms. Evans. So, which is it? You lied about having a personal loyalty card—or you recognize this card as belonging to TSS?"

It took Mallory less than a second to decide she was loyal—to herself. "I recognize it as the group card. There's a tear on right side. And a blue mark in the middle."

"How do we find out who used the card last?" asked Dom.

Mallory sighed heavily. "We keep it in the common area in the main building. Anyone can take it if it's available. We don't have a sign-out sheet or anything, but Harry will probably know who used it last."

DOMINIC HANDED ME A Cherry Dr. Pepper while we waited for Connelly to drop Mallory Evans off at her cell and bring us Gary Davis for the next interview. "You've got good instincts, Nicole. You did well—even if you did jump the gun."

"Sorry about that." I popped the top on the can and took a drink. The sweet carbonation burned its way down my dry throat. "Thanks for the Coke."

"That's not Coke. Did you want a Coke? I can get that for you instead."

"Down in these parts if it's a carbonated beverage it's a Coke." I chuckled. "It's like saying soda or pop or soda pop. It's all-encompassing."

"Why is that?"

"Ah, the sweet mysteries of life." I took another sip. "Mallory's not a psycho. Well, I guess I should amend that to say she doesn't have APD. She's her own special kind of crazy."

"She didn't exactly look away from the photos," mused Dom. "But shifters are used to the more brutal sides of life. What do you think?"

"She's reactive. Impulsive. If she was our killer, I think the crimes would be a lot messier—and not as well planned. Our suspect is an organized killer. He has to watch his targets for a while, get a feel for their routines. Then he figures out where best to grab them."

"If Ms. Evans is any indication of the caliber of TSS members," said Dom. "I'm not real hopeful the other two will be our killer, either. "

I finished off the can and belched. Oh, God. I died a little inside. "My bad." I waved at the air in front of my mouth. I felt my face warm. Ugh.

Dominic laughed. "That's disgusting."

"As Mom would say, so not attractive."

"Your mom says that?"

I shrugged. "I'm paraphrasing."

"For the record, you could fart and still be attractive."

"That's disgusting," I said.

He laughed again, and the sound sent shivers up and down my spine. God, he had was too freaking handsome and funny and charming for my own good. My body language must have reflected my romantic thoughts because Dominic took a step toward me. He reached up and stroked a stray lock of hair back behind my ear. My body clenched with pleasure.

I sidestepped and turned my back to him afraid my lusty thoughts would be written all over my face. "I think we should stake out the compound."

"You're still bothered by how easily the TSS handed over our suspects."

"Doesn't it bother you?"

"They might thumb their noses at the FBI," he said, "but they're not stupid enough to defy the Tri-Council."

"Maybe. I think they're hiding something. But it might not have anything to do with our case." I pivoted back toward Dominic. He was leaning back on the interview desk, his long legs stretched, and his arms crossed over his chest. My throat went dry. Damn, I needed another Coke. "Maybe I should go alone." I shook my head. "I mean, I can take Eldin. He can help me identify the people going in and out of the compound. It's practical."

Dominic's expression darkened. "Practical. Right."

"It's just an idea."

Connelly knocked on the open door. He guided Gary Davis, a short, stocky man with chestnut brown hair into the room. After he got him seated on the suspect side of the interview table, he nodded to Dom and me. "Holler when you're finished."

I nodded back. "Thanks, Michael."

Dominic closed the door after Connelly left the room, and we both took our places on the other side.

Unlike Mallory, Gary was unruffled. Stoic, even. "I haven't been to Springfield in two years," he said before we could ask our first question. "On the night in question, I was at home watching a *Mission Impossible* marathon on US TV with my wife."

"Really? Which movie were you watching when the storm knocked out the power?"

He frowned. "What the hell are you talking about it? The power never went out."

Hmm. I leaned forward. "Well, your alibi is easy enough to check out. We'll talk to your wife. Verify US TV ran a movie marathon of Mission Impossible movies."

Davis started tapping his thumb against the table. "I didn't do anything." He sounded uncertain, nervous.

"We never said you did," said Dom coolly.

"Then why am I here?"

"Because we have evidence you dropped the TSS loyalty card at a crime scene."

"I told you. I wasn't in Springfield."

"What makes you think the crime happened in Springfield?" asked Dom.

Gary leaned back and crossed his arms. "It's a small town—news travel fast, especially when human law enforcement starts sniffing around. Those shifter murders aren't exactly top secret. Even the humans know about the Little Piggy serial killer. And we know that some guy was abducted in Springfield."

"Not just a guy. An integrator."

I watched Gary's expression turned to disgust. He curled his lip. "Shifters are the superior species. It's downright shameful to watch our own kind mix with humans. Integrators will be the downfall of the therians—just you wait." Gary gave us both the evil eye. "I don't know anything. And I didn't do anything."

"I think we're done here," Dominic said. "If we have any more questions for you, Mr. Davis, we have your number."

Gary relaxed, but his gaze was still distrustful. "Can I go home?"

Dom looked at me. I nodded. He got up and opened the door. "Deputy, can you go ahead and get the release paperwork ready for Mr. Davis?"

After the Davis was taken from the room, Dom said, "You tried to trip him up with that power outage question. I'm impressed."

"Be impressed with my mother. It's her technique. If I said I was at my friend Cynthia Stinger's house, but Mom thought I was trying to sneak off with a boy, she'd say something like, 'I ran into Cynthia's parents at the market, and they said they had a power outage at their house. That must have been awful.' And if I said, the power never went out, then she would say, oh, maybe it happened on a different day."

Dom raised his brow at me. "Your mom invented her own lie detector test."

"Yeah. If I hadn't been at my friend's, I would have said something like, oh yeah, it really sucked, and she would have me cold—and I'd be grounded till kingdom come."

"Your mom should have gone into law enforcement."

I grinned. "My dad says the same thing."

"Davis didn't bite, though,, so we're presuming he's telling the truth."

I nodded. "For now."

Connelly escorted in Tolliver. The man's thick blond hair was choppily cut, and he had an unruly beard that reached his chest. He looked angry. I knew immediately he wouldn't fall for a "Mom special."

He was forcibly placed in the chair, and I noticed a red bump rising on Connelly's forehead. The deputy grumbled. "He surprised me."

"Did he hit you?" I gave Tolliver a look that I hoped

conveyed just how stupid I thought he was for assaulting a police officer at a police station.

Connelly grimaced. "He tripped me and hit my head on the cell bars." The deputy gave the prisoner a quick, light slap against the back of his head. "Behave," he said as a final warning then took his leave.

Dom and I sat down across from him. Dom took the lead.

"Mister Tolliver, can you tell us where you were three nights ago?"

His response was an abrupt, "No."

I hadn't resistance after the first two interviews. This could be interesting. I nudged Dom and pointed to my folded list of questions.

He nodded. "Mister Tolliver, do you consider yourself an honest man?"

Tolliver looked surprised. "Uhm, sure. I guess so." The first question was just to throw him off balance.

Dom put his elbows on the table. "Did you play sports in high school?"

I loved that my partner didn't even blink as he asked. Tolliver tugged at the bottom of his shirt. His shoulder movement indicated he was wringing his hands. "I...I, no, but I don't see what that has to do with anything."

Defensive. Interesting. This guy was insecure.

"What did you have for breakfast yesterday?"

He tucked his chin. "A bowl of cinnamon and raisin oatmeal, a cup of skim milk, and dry wheat toast." He glared at Dominic. "The doc says my blood pressure is too high."

Dominic glanced at me. That was my last question. I wanted to get a baseline for how he responded to a question that required details and description.

"I like cinnamon raisin oatmeal," I said.

"Good for you," Tolliver responded. "When can I get out of here?"

"As soon as you answer our first question. Where were you three nights ago?"

"I've been answering." He threw up his hands. "Fine. Home. I ate dinner and went to bed early."

"What did you eat?"

"Do you have a food fetish or something?"

"Answer her question." Dom's voice was the scary kind of quiet, and Tolliver noticed.

"I ate pork chops."

I shook my head. "I don't believe you, Mister Tolliver." I looked at Dominic. "I think he needs more time to think about his alibi."

Sweat darkened Tolliver's T-shirt. "I don't need a freakin' alibi."

"Your prints were found at the scene of an abduction—three nights ago."

"That's...no. I...who was abducted? Someone in town?" He rubbed his face. "Jesus. I'm all over this town for supplies and such. I don't kidnap folks."

"Then where were you?" I pressed. The fact that he thought the abduction took place in Peculiar told me that he probably wasn't our culprit.

"Son of a bitch. If I tell you, you can't tell anyone."

"If it's not pertinent to the case, there won't be any need to share the information publicly."

Tolliver rubbed his face again then wiped his fingers on his pants. "I was with someone...married."

I fought a gasp because at the heart of the matter I was still a small-town girl and this was juicy gossip. *I will not tell Mom. I will not tell Mom*, I repeated to myself. "Will this person vouch for you?"

He shrugged. "I think so. But don't approach her with people around, please."

"I promise." I crossed my heart.

Tolliver nodded. "It's Audrey Halliver."

I fought off another gasp. Audrey and her husband Halliver owned Halliver's Hilltop Motel. Did he and Audrey do it in one of the rooms? *I will not tell Mom. I will not tell Mom.*

"You'll stay in custody until we verify what you've told us."

Tolliver nodded.

"Okay, then." Dom pushed back from the table and stood up. "Be nice to Deputy Connelly, or you might end up staying another night on principle."

When the room was cleared, I sagged against the wall. "That was a colossal waste of time."

"Lunch?" Dom asked as he packed away the case files.

"Sure."

Connelly knocked outside the open door and poked his head in the room. "Something's happened."

"What's up?" I asked.

"Brandon Messer just showed up with his dad."

Connelly shook his head. "Brandon found a dead body near his trailer."

"Did he know who it was?"

Connelly took a deep breath and blew it out noisily. "He's real shook-up. I don't think he got more than a peek."

"If it's Lieberman, it'll support our theory that the killer lives in Peculiar."

I didn't want to believe anyone I knew was capable of being the Little Piggy murderer. "The unsub dumps the bodies at their homes. Dumping a body here would be completely off script." I looked at Connelly. "Where's Dad?"

"Sheriff Taylor is already on his way."

Dominic strolled toward the door, his body charged with raw energy. "We're going too."

Connelly stepped out in front of him. "Sheriff Taylor says that until they know who the victim is, this is town business, not FBI business."

"Then file it under Tri-Council business. Every therian death falls under my jurisdiction."

I looked at the squirrel shifter who was standing between a rock and a hard man. "Look, Michael. I know this involves your in-laws. You should go be with Roger and Brandon until we get back. Roger's probably a wreck."

Connelly's eyes reddened. "Selena keeps calling and texting me. I'm worried this stress is going to affect her pregnancy."

"Then you need to do what you can to protect her

brother." I put my hand on his forearm. "You may not trust my partner but trust me."

He stepped back from the door. I looked past him to Dominic, who had waited for me with his back turned. He'd heard what I'd said to the scared deputy. "Thanks. It'll be okay."

"No, it won't," said Connelly, "but thanks for saying it."

CHAPTER ELEVEN

*W*e got the address and headed out to the crime scene. Doc Smith was there, along with Mark Smart, the coroner and the owner of the local funeral home. My dad wore a grim expression as he knelt down next to the body. Two pale, naked feet stuck out from under the tarp. Was that how Brandon had found it? I didn't believe the man had anything to do with this particular death. If he did, he'd be up for the Darwin Award for what not to do when you're trying to get away with murder.

Dom simmered with anger on the way over, and he'd barely spoken two words to me. I think my dad trying to keep us from the scene burned his ass a little. I think because I wasn't mad made him even more irritated. I didn't agree with him, so I would have to let him calm down on his own. It wasn't in me to try and placate his mood.

"Is it Lieberman?" Dom asked first thing.

Doctor Smith answered. "No. It's Lloyd Evans."

The blood drained from my face, leaving me cold. He'd been a cantankerous ass, but it still punched me in the gut that I knew the person laying at our feet. "We saw him last night. What the hell happened in the last twelve hours?"

"Good question." Dad nodded at Doc Smith. "How long would you say he's been dead?"

The tall, silver-haired werewolf knelt down. "The cold weather we had last night skews the time, but I'd hazard a guess between eight and twelve hours based on the lack of rigor."

"Any idea on the cause of death?"

"He has abrasions on his arms, legs, and the bottom of his feet. There's a laceration on his left hand and three on his torso. He has a nasty wound on the back of his head. Right now, it looks like the head wound might've been the fatal blow. "

"Minimal blood," said Dom, studying the body. "None on the tarp, either."

"Rain might've washed it away," said Dad.

"Or he'd been dead a few hours before getting dumped here."

The doctor shifted the tarp so we could see Lloyd's upper body. "I think you're right, Agent Tartan." He pointed to Lloyd's left cheek, shoulder, and the side of this arm. "You see how this is all dark here from where the blood has pooled. That's caused from being on his left side when he died. He was found on his back. I looked, and there aren't any dark areas there."

Dom scanned the ground. "The killer didn't do that great of a job hiding the corpse."

"If Evans wasn't killed here, then the murderer chose to put his body near Brandon's trailer," said Dad. "And used the woodpile tarp to cover it up."

"Unless Brandon did it, and he's trying to make out like he found the body," pointed out Dom. "Maybe he was the one who put it here."

"But why cover the body if the killer wanted it to be discovered?" I agreed with Dom. There wasn't any evidence that Evans met his demise here. But I had an idea about the tarp. "I think whoever put that tarp on Evans knew him. There's psychological precedence for this behavior. A killer will cover up a body out of a sense of shame and guilt. They literally can't look at the face of the person they've killed."

"Well, he's still got his pinky toes, so I think this might be a local matter." Dad stood up.

"We're still part of this investigation," I said to my dad. "Evans may not be the victim we're looking for, but we spoke to him last night in connection with our case, and today he turns up dead? It's too big to dismiss as a coincidence."

"I'm with Agent Taylor on this." Dominic used my title, I was certain, to remind my dad that I was a trained law enforcement agent.

"If we discover that this crime has nothing to do with yours, then I hope you'll take a step back. There's no sense in muddying the waters of your investigation with another crime that's not connected."

"Agreed," I said, trying not to go up on my toes in triumph. I failed. My dad gave me a surly look. He was all too familiar with my victory stance.

"Well, Nicole," Dom said. "You wanted to investigate the TSS more. Lloyd Evans has just given you the keys to the kingdom. Poor bastard."

"Doc." I walked over the Doctor Smith. "You said there is a laceration on Lloyd's left hand and three on his torso."

"Yes." His gray eyes assessed me. "What are you thinking?"

"If I gave you photos of the wounds on our previous victims, do you think there is any way to tell if these cuts were made by the same weapon?"

"That's a tough one. I wouldn't be able to say with any certainty, but I could give you a best guess." He chewed his lower lip for a moment. He really was a nice-looking man. I could see why Chavvah was gaga for him, much the way I was gaga for he-who-shall-not-be-named. And with my hands at my sides, I could literally feel Dom's presence right behind me.

I looked over my shoulder. "Can we get the autopsy photos for the doc?"

"Sure," Dom said. He nodded to Doctor Smith. "I heard you say you wouldn't be able to tell if it's the same sharp tool or knife, but do you think you might be able to tell if the wounds were made by the same person?"

"Not exactly," Doc said, his deep voice rumbling. "But it might be possible to determine if the same weapon was used—and if it was used with the same amount of force ."

"Thanks," I said. "I appreciate it. This case is coming

up cold. We have a missing man that I don't know if he is dead or alive, and this body is the only thing we've come up against that resembles a viable clue." My frustration level rose. What if the loyalty card had nothing to do with the kidnapping—or with the Little Piggy killer? We could be on a wild goose chase while Lieberman was getting tortured.

Dominic's hands went to my shoulders, his fingers gently digging into my knotted muscles. "We'll get him," he said reassuringly.

I closed my eyes for only the briefest moment before I moved away. The last thing I needed was to look like I couldn't handle myself. "Thanks," I muttered to Dominic. Maybe he could show me what those magic fingers could do later.

Deputy Thompson, who had been searching behind the woodpile, waved at my dad. "Sheriff, I found something."

"What is it?" Dominic stepped around me toward the deputy. "What did you find?"

Under the tarp on the backside of the pile, was a wooden crate. "I'm not sure what's in it, but it's hidden, and it's got a padlock on it. Seems pretty suspicious to me."

"Get it open," my dad said. "If it's something personal that's none of our business, we'll apologize and buy Brandon a new lock."

My excitement level upped a notch when I saw the padlock. "That's a combination lock."

"Yep, and it's titanium," Deputy Thompson said. "Those are hard as hell to break."

"But easy to crack," I said.

"You know how to crack a combination lock?" Dom asked.

"I do. I also know how to pick a lot of locks. I have a rack, a pick, and locking wrench in my purse." I grinned.

"I like a woman who's always prepared," Dom said in my ear.

"Then you're gonna love me." I blushed, wishing I could take back the words as soon as they came out of my mouth.

"You know," Dom replied. "I think I really could."

I met his gaze, but before I could respond with what I am sure would have amounted to inane bluster, my dad saved me by saying, "Well, get it open, Puddin'."

Noooooooo. Leave it to my dad to kill my really cool moment. "Okay. Give me room."

My dad opened a bottle of water as I went by and I held out my hands while he sprinkled some on my fingers. I pushed my beast, eager and curious forward, just a little, just enough to activate the superfine hairs that act as direct messengers to my brain. Instantly, the cold breeze was sharper and my energy hyper-focused. I could break the combination lock without the extra sensitivity, but with my raccoon's help, I could do it under ten seconds.

I went to my knees in front of the box. I tugged on the lock a couple of time then turned the dial to the right three times and set it to zero. Next, I gently pulled down on the lock to put tension in the neck and slowly turned the dial right against the resistance. Soon, the resistance eased and then locked at twenty-four. I beamed with satisfaction. I did the same to the left until it locked. Sixteen. Last, I went right with it again and waited for the number to lock. Seven. I pulled down on the lock, and it popped. I turned the cylinder out and slid the lock from its latch holding the crate shut.

"Bravo," Dominic said. "I'm impressed. You learn that in your doctorate's program?"

His teasing voice made me squirm. "I learned that when I forgot the combination to my locker at school."

"You are a constant surprise, Nicole." Dominic's eyes softened at the corners. "Constant."

"Impressive," Doc Smith said. He was not only the town physician, but he was also a spiritual leader in our community, and his approval filled me with pride.

Thompson opened the box lid and was scooping away loose hay that had been placed inside. "Sheriff, this box is full of semi-automatic rifles."

I looked down. I wasn't familiar with the model. "What kind of guns are those?"

"Those," Dom said as he picked one up from the box, "are M16 A4 rifles. Military issue. Soon to be retired. Why in the hell are they in a box behind a trailer in Peculiar?"

CHAPTER TWELVE

"*I* had no idea there was a box of rifles in my backyard," Brandon Messer said. His eyes had the wild twitch of a captured animal. "Just like I didn't know about the body. Why would I come to the police if I had anything to hide?"

"People with nothing to hide don't run from questioning," my dad said.

My dad hadn't wanted Dominic to question Brandon, not until he knew more information about the current murder. His only concession was allowing me to be in the room. I was supposed to "keep my lips buttoned," but I was never any good at the quiet game. I narrowed my gaze at Brandon. "You warned Mallory Evans your parent's restaurant, and then you took off before we could talk to you. Now her cousin Lloyd is dead. None of this says, innocent."

Brandon slapped the table, and I flinched. His words

were pleading. "You know me, Nic. You have to believe me. I wouldn't kill anyone."

I didn't believe him. Brandon had a temper in high school, and given the right circumstances, anyone could be a killer. However, I didn't think he'd killed Lloyd. He'd have to have the I.Q. of a gnat to move a dead body from an original crime scene to his backyard. "What about the guns, Brandon? You can't tell me you didn't know about the crate."

"Look, I went out to get some chopped wood for my wood stove and there he was."

"And you called your dad, not the police."

"I was going to call you, but Dad showed up right after I found Lloyd. I didn't call him. He insisted we come to the station. He said Sheriff Taylor would help clear me."

"You can't clear someone who's guilty," my dad said, but I was still stuck on the fact that Brandon hadn't called his father. It made me wonder if he would have called anyone if his dad hadn't shown up at his home. And, how long before his dad arrived had he discovered the body?

I tapped the table to draw his attention. "When did you find Lloyd?"

Brandon stared at me. "I told you. My dad got there about eleven o'clock. It was right before that."

"And what was your first reaction?" I waved my hand in a rolling gesture. "You know, to finding a dead man."

"I...terrible, of course. I mean, you know, I was scared. It really freaked me out."

"And what did you do next?"

"I'm not sure what you mean."

"I mean," I said, staring him dead in the eye. "What did you do immediately after pulling the tarp back and finding that body, Brandon. What next?"

"I…"

"Did you call someone? If we dump your phone records are we going to see calls that took place from the time you discovered the body until your dad showed up at eleven?"

"I don't know. I don't remember making any calls." He looked frightened beyond the prospect of going to jail. Was he scared of something else? Someone else?

"Did you hit your head, Brandon? Is this selective amnesia? Because I'm a psychologist, and I can tell you, I'm not buying your "I don't know anything" act. What are you hiding?"

My dad gave me a look of reassessment as if he'd never seen me before.

Brandon started crying. It shocked me enough to consider backing off, but I pressed on. "If you are scared of someone, we can protect you, Brandon. We can keep you safe."

"No, you can't," Brandon said. "Why did I come back here? I shouldn't have come back." He covered his face with his hands. "I'm not saying anymore." He put his hands down and looked at me, his red-rimmed eyes begging for this all to be over. "I've told you everything I know."

I glanced at my dad. "I think it's time we looked at his call logs."

The door opened to the interrogation room. Deputy Boden lead with her stomach through the door. "Andy Lark is here, and he insists that he is Brandon's lawyer."

I looked at Brandon. "Is that true?" It seemed awfully convenient that Andy showed up to save the day. "Did you call him?"

Brandon's shoulders rounded as he hunched forward. Andy Lark was suddenly behind Willy in the doorway. "He called me right after he gave you all his statement earlier. He has the right to counsel."

Willy rounded on him, her belly shoving him back. "You don't get to come in here until I tell you, buddy. You got that?"

Andy put his hands up, taken aback by the pregnant surprise attack. "Pardon me."

"I'll pardon my foot up your ass if you don't get it back in the bullpen."

His nearly colorless eyes widened indignantly. "I have a right to be with my client."

My dad held up his hand. Let him in, Deputy Boden. We'll take it from here."

"You got it, Sheriff." She postured at Andy and made him jump back. This made her giggle hard enough she tooted on the way out without even a second glance back.

I focused on the situation. Dead man. Guns. Assholes. All to keep myself from busting out laughing the very pregnant and gassy deputy, who could probably take out Andy and Brandon without blinking.

Andy took the seat next to Brandon. "How you holding up?" he asked.

Brandon nodded but didn't look at him.

"Good. Don't say any more than you already have. That's what I'm here for."

I pursed my lips and glared at Lark. "You're an attorney?" I asked, unable to keep the incredulity from my voice.

Andy produced a business card, *Andy Lark, LLC. Attorney at Law.* "I am the legal counsel for TSS and all its members."

I turned to the scared bear shifter. "Is this true, Brandon? Are you a member of TSS?" He'd been an integrator, so it was hard to see him as a prepper.

"I'm in-process," he admitted. "I haven't been accepted yet."

"Yes, you have," Andy said. He put his hand on Brandon's shoulder. "You are one of us. And we take care of our own."

My dad leaned back in his chair, crossing his arms over his chest. "If Brandon has nothing to hide, then he should have no problem answering our questions."

"Sid, you and I both know that what you're saying is absolutely not true. Innocent people are convicted of crimes every day. Only, when you're an innocent therianthrope convicted of the crime of murder, you don't get an appeal. I won't let that happen to my client."

"Well, Andy," Dad said, making use of Lark's first name in the same condescending way. "Your showing up here makes me want to question you and everyone out on that compound of yours. Which, would be my prerogative, considering the dead guy is also a member of the TSS."

"All that means is that the death is even more tragic. Lloyd Evans was an important member of our movement. There is no one who wants to see his killer brought to justice more than me. You're just crawling into the wrong garbage can with your current suspect."

When I was in school, I'd heard my fair share of raccoon jokes, especially by the larger predators. Andy's plain features made it impossible to tell what kind of animal lurked beneath his smarmy surface. And his super pale eyes confused me even more. I'd thought he might be an opossum before but with that last predatory remark of his, I wasn't sure.

I leaned sideways toward my dad and whispered conspiratorially, "Sheriff Taylor, is this douchebag being speciest? Is that what I'm hearing?"

"I don't think so, Agent Taylor. I don't think he's stupid enough to walk into my station and start handing out insults."

"Now, now," Andy said. "I apologize if you thought I was being rude. I meant no disrespect."

"In other words," I told my dad. "He's only sorry if we're mad. Which means," I spread my hands apart, "not sorry."

Brandon groaned. "This just keeps getting worse and worse."

The corner of my dad's mouth tugged up a little. "You can always get another lawyer."

Dominic entered the room holding a file. "It's amazing what a few phone calls will get you." He put the file down on the table. "You were in the Army," he said to Brandon.

"Oh, yeah. Dad told me you were in the Army. When did you get out?"

"I was honorably discharged last year."

I remembered Dominic saying at the crime scene that the rifles had been military issue. "Then you know what an M16 A4 rifle is then."

Brandon shrugged.

"I'll take that as a yes."

My dad scooted the file over in front of him and said, "Thank you, Special Agent Tartan," without ever looking up at Dom.

My partner looked as surprised as I felt. My dad had just dismissed him. With prejudice.

The look Dominic gave me right before he exited said that I was in for a long talk later. I put my focus where it belonged. "What did you do for them, Brandon? The Army, I mean."

"Infantry." He frowned. "Why?"

"That's not the only thing, though, right?" Dom asked. "You trained to be a Ranger, didn't you?"

Brandon slunk further down in his seat. It was weird watching such a big man trying to make himself so small.

"It's too bad you failed out. Your Drill Instructor said you showed a lot of promise until the water training."

He scooted sideways in his chair. "I get claustrophobic." He lowered his head. "My unit chased an Afghanistan warlord into a mountain cave. It was full of these aqueducts. We got pinned down in the water for three days." He shuddered. "I thought I could do it. But I couldn't get past it in Ranger training." His body language had turned from defensive to shame. "It's why I got out."

Now, I felt bad. Brandon "Did you see any VA counselors?"

Brandon flexed his fists. "I'm done. I didn't do anything. I didn't kill Lloyd, and I want to go home."

My dad shook his head. "I'm sorry, Brandon. I can't do that. You are being detained until we can further determine what if any role you played in the death and why there was a case of automatic rifles near the scene."

"You can't hold me without charging me," Brandon said.

Lark furrowed his brow and scratched his forehead. "Actually, Brandon, they can. Via article twenty-five b of criminal acts involving suspicious death."

"That's not a thing," he said. "I haven't even had my rights read to me."

"You seem to forget that this isn't a human jail, Brandon," my dad said gently. "We adhere to human laws insomuch as we don't want to violate them and have a shapeshifter wind up in a human jail. That would be bad for everyone. What your attorney is quoting to you is the legal canon for therianthropes. You've been gone too long, son. We have our own set of rules, and we have to stick to them." My dad looked at me. "Do you want to explain why?"

I felt as if he were testing me. Would his integrator daughter understand why therianthropes would have fewer rights than a human? Of course, I did. I didn't like it, but I understood. "Brandon, you know that therians can't afford to allow murder suspects a chance to escape. Not into human populations. Keeping you in jail until we sort this out is for the safety of us all."

It surprised me to see Andy Lark nodding his head.

"Agent Taylor is absolutely right." He patted Brandon on the back. "I don't believe you're guilty, Brandon. Not one bit. But the law is the law." He turned his creepy gaze on us, and it made me shiver. "Brandon may not have the right to leave, but he does have a right to keep his mouth shut. You are finished with my client for the day."

My dad sighed. "I'll have Deputy Thompson escort him to a cell." Then I saw my dad do something uncharacteristic for his interactions with a suspect. He leaned across the table and put his hand on Brandon's arm in a gesture of comfort. "I'll tell your folks what's going on. I don't know if you had anything to do with the murder. I sure hope not. There is no coming back from that. What I do know is that you're into something. Something murky and you are neck deep. I'm afraid for you, son. I'm afraid you're going to drown. I don't want to see that. Not for your parents. Not for your sister. Not for you. When you wise up, you tell whoever is on duty to call me."

Brandon's eyes were stark as he looked at my dad. For a moment, I thought he would spill everything he was hiding, but a shoulder squeeze from Lark kept Brandon buttoned up.

Thompson came and got him. Lark escorted his client out. I looked at dad. "What in the world was all that?"

"Nothing good, Puddin'. Nothing good."

"Dad," I whined, annoying myself even more. "You have to stop calling me Puddin' while I'm on the job. It's undermining any authority I have."

My dad frowned then suck his teeth. "You and Agent Tartan sure seem cozy."

"When did you turn into Mom?" Dad had never been interested in my love life or lack thereof. He'd always seemed perfectly happy to pretend I was asexual. "Why all the sudden interest?"

"No interest," Dad said with a certain nonchalance that bordered on boredom.

I wasn't buying it. "Senior Special Agent Tartan, emphasis on the senior, is my partner and superior." I grimaced at the word. "In rank only, mind you."

Dad smirked. "There's my tough girl."

"Hush. I'm just trying to say that there is nothing going on between us that isn't purely professional."

Dad picked up the file Dom brought in straightened by dropping the edge onto the desk as he held it closed. He gave me a sly look and said, "If you say so, Puddin'."

I clenched my teeth as I stalked past him to the door. "Stop. Calling. Me. Puddin'."

CHAPTER THIRTEEN

*D*om and I sat in our unmarked sedan about three miles outside the TSS compound off the road in a thicket of trees. If someone wasn't directly looking when they passed, we would go unnoticed. The early afternoon had been intense around the sheriff's department. Dom had called a military liaison and gave him serial numbers on the weapons. If we could track them back their origin, we might be able to pin down the seller and buyer, though I was certain we already had the buyer in custody. Dominic had barely said two words to me that weren't work-related, and frankly, it was started to raise my blood pressure.

Dom cocked his head to the side and looked down at my waist. "What is that thing, again?"

"It's a fanny pack for Christ sake. It's not like it's a new invention." Was my reaction strong? Yes. Had he already asked me this question? Yes. Three times. I think he just liked hearing me say "fanny pack." "It's handier than my purse when breaking and entering." I unzipped the pack. "See," I held up a multi-tool. "This has a blade, a wrench, a Phillips and flat head screwdriver, wire cutters, and pliers." I put it back and withdrew a small pouch. "This is my lock picking kit." I withdrew the other items one at a time. "A thumb light, Chapstick, hair scrunchie, and hand wipes. All the necessities."

"You could have been a scout."

I rolled my eyes, showed him the whites, and then sighed. "We're no closer to finding Lieberman or this mysterious Little Piggy guy. If the Lieberman is still alive, he is suffering. I don't know what to do next, Dom. The punch card has turned into a dead end."

"Maybe." He stared out at the road.

Judge Holt was signing a warrant for us to search the compound tomorrow, but we were afraid if the preppers found out, they would move things before we could find whatever they might be hiding. So, here we sat, watching for suspicious vehicles going in and out of the compound while we waited for dark so we could illegally sneak around the wall, gain entrance somehow, and have a quiet look around. It went against my training as an FBI agent, but it played right into my strengths as a sneak. Raccoons were naturally curious, and our animal's nature had a habit of getting us into situations that most people would avoid. Like trespassing on property that was occupied by, most likely, well-armed paranoid therians with severe trust issues.

And even though I had agreed to not tell my dad or

anyone else, Dominic still acted mad at me. "What is going on with you?"

"Nothing," he said. He took a double twist glazed donut from a box that had Sunny's Outlook written on the side then took a sip of his coffee.

"You've hardly said a word to me all day."

"I just said a word before you said that. And there, I just said a bunch more." He took another bite, his jaw flexing as he chewed.

"Just tell me why you're mad, so I can apologize already."

He stopped chewing and looked at me. "You're the new agent, Nicole, not me. So when your dad dismisses me from an interview as if I'm nothing more than an errand boy, it irritates me. You, however, have nothing to apologize for. I'm not mad at you."

"Could've fooled me," I grumbled.

Dom's brow wrinkled with irritation. He put the half-eaten donut back into the box, rubbed his hands together, releasing sugary crumbs onto his jeans. God, he had thickly muscled thighs the size of tree trunks. Tree trunks I wanted to straddle. I swallowed the lump in my throat.

"Keep looking at me like that, partner, and it's going to be impossible to keep this professional."

His glib reply knocked the lusty thoughts right out of me. "Look, buddy. Raccoons might have a reputation for being promiscuous and indiscriminate, but if you think I'm going to have quick, meaningless sex with you, you are mistaken."

"I never said anything about the sex being meaningless." He stretched. "And it definitely wouldn't be quick."

There was no way to respond to his claim that wouldn't fall into the realm of foreplay. Instead, I took a deep breath and dragged my fingertips across my jeans. The texture against my skin helped calm my nerves and my hormones. "Do you think Lieberman is in there? Behind the wall somewhere on that compound?"

"Maybe." He sat up straight. "Okay, Doctor Taylor. You've had a chance to meet several people we believe have ties to our killer. So, if we were playing the suspect game, who makes the list and who doesn't?"

Shop talk I could do. "Brandon Messer, our suspect in custody, is low on my list."

"Because he's an old friend?"

"No, because he's a hot mess. He is clearly suffering from post-traumatic stress disorder. He's disorganized. Did you see his trailer? That is not a guy who is giving much thought to his next shower, let alone his next kill. No. If it turned out to be Brandon, I'd turn in my badge and move back in with my parents."

"Okay. Next person. Do you think Lloyd Evans could have been the killer and somebody got him before we could? Meting out a little therian justice before we get a chance?"

I wrinkled my nose and shook my head. "Lloyd had enough rage to kill. I believe that, but he's impulsive. The way he kicked the chair across the floor. No. I think our killer is cool, calm and collected. I don't think Lloyd was a serial killer, but I'm not discounting that his death could be related to our investigation."

"Andy Lark."

"Oh, I like that guy for a killer. He definitely has the confidence, the intellect, the lack of empathy, and he's organized. The way he breezed in today and sabotaged our interrogation with Brandon was calculated. However, he's a lawyer."

"What's that mean?"

"Personality can dictate occupation, and often does. And as I've said before, psychopaths lack empathy, they are goal oriented, high organized planners, and these characteristics that make hard to catch killers also makes skilled lawyers, big business CEOs, and politicians. It's easy to be ruthless and cutthroat when you don't care." I held up a finger. "I'll amend that, when you can't care, at least not about other people."

"So, he could be our guy."

I shrugged. "Maybe. Or he could just be a royal ass. Not all psychopaths are murderers. Some are just morally ambiguous jerks."

Dom's mouth twitched. "You're pretty smart."

"Are you surprised?"

"Not at all." He rotated at the waist to face me. His broad shoulders blocked the light coming in from the afternoon sun. It made him appear as if he had a halo outlining his head. "What do you see when you look at me?"

"You are competent, intelligent, and driven."

"Come on, Nic. You can do better than that."

It was hard to concentrate when his pale green eyes staring at me. "You have a flirtatious personality. Playful. You approach flirting with someone else as a game. If the person responds, you win. You know you're handsome. You know you have a pleasing physique. You've probably had women throwing themselves at you since puberty, but you enjoy the chase. You are confident, but you have commitment issues. I think you enjoy the pursuit more than the catch. Divorced parents. Lots of moving around when you were growing up. It can make it hard to trust anyone."

Dom's expression darkened. His head tilted to the side. His low voice had a growly undercurrent. "Is that really how you see me?"

"I don't know." I gulped. "Maybe."

His mouth thinned for a moment then he grinned. "You think I'm handsome and have a pleasing physique. Good to know."

"Of course, those are the two things you latched onto."

He shrugged, a smug look on his face. "It was the only two accurate things you said." He winked. "Except the chase part. I do like a good chase."

Time to change the subject. "I wish we knew more about what motivates our unsub."

"Well, we know, thanks to you, that all the victims were integrators. That ties in the TSS connection. Those guys definitely see humans as the enemies and integrators as traitors."

"There could be someone on that compound that we haven't met yet who has Lieberman locked up down his basement. It might not be anyone we've come across yet."

Dom put his hand out to quiet me. "I hear a vehicle coming."

The road was gravel and full of potholes, which made it impossible to go more than twenty or thirty miles an hour. Not if you didn't want holes in your exhaust or oil pan. When I saw the burgundy truck and the bearded man behind the wheel, my pulse kicked up a notch.

"This isn't going to be good."

"What?" Dom asked. "Who was that?"

"That was Homer Halliver. I have a bad feeling someone leaked the news that his wife and Darrel Tolliver have been seeing each other naked."

"Craptastic."

"Yep," I agreed. "Shit. I bet you dollars to donuts we're about to get overrun with Sheriff vehicles."

Fifteen minutes later, a parade of lights and sirens screamed passed us.

"Should we join them?"

I was in jeans, a black T-shirt, and a fuzzy lined black hoodie, and damn it, I wanted to search the compound. "If Dad calls we'll go. If he doesn't, I say we use my dad and his deputies as a distraction and sneak in now."

Dom had a glint in his eye when he looked at me. "Nicole Taylor, I like the way you think."

We got out of the car and headed off into the woods, casting a wide path around the enclosed compound. I'd found out about a stream that crossed the property, and we walked until we ran into it and followed it up toward the compound. Crap. The culvert had a wire grate in place at the bottom to keep woodland critters out. The gray afternoon sky made the woods shadowy. It made it difficult to distinguish one dark area from the other. I stopped, and Dom raised a questioning brow.

"The stream," I said quietly. We approached slowly ready to bolt if we activated any motion sensors. I pointed at the grate. "I know there's a grate there, but I want to check if there's a weak spot. It could be our way in."

"That water has to be freezing," he protested.

I stuck my finger in. "I'd say it's about forty-eight degrees. Not freezing."

"Cold enough."

"Wait here and hibernate. I'm going to check it out." The moving water flowed away from the compound. Good. It meant there wouldn't be a lot of debris on this side of the screen. The idea of touching every squishy, nasty rotting branch, leaves, insects, or small dead animals didn't excite me one bit. So, the flow worked in my favor.

I took off my jacket, my boots, and socks, rolled up my jeans to my knees, and prepared to get wet.

"You're not really going down there, are you?" Dom's low voice, even in a whisper, carried.

"Hush now." I stepped into the chilly stream, the water shocking my warm toes. "The point is to sneak in. Or are you hoping for an invitation into the backdoor?"

He quirked his upper lip. "I've charmed my way into a few backdoors."

I snarled. "Ew. I don't want to hear about your conquests. It's gross." My feet adjusted to the cold as I waded in deeper.

"Now, Nic," he said. "I didn't mean it like that."

"Whatever. Just keep a lookout. The grate goes down several feet. I'll explore it for an entry point."

Dom moved closer to me and the culvert. "If you find it, do you honestly expect me to go through there? One, it's cold. I told you, bears don't like the cold. And second, I am not a small man, if you haven't noticed, so why you may be able to squeeze your skinny, albeit cute, butt through there, it will be impossible for me to do so."

We needed to get inside. The razor wire and motion-activated security lights made sneaking over the wall impossible, and this stream was our best bet on getting in unseen. "I'll go in without you."

"Bullshit. You know the drill. FBI protocol requires us to stay together. Agents who go, cowboy, get killed. Besides that, I'm the senior agent, and you're the trainee, which you are fond of forgetting. This is a no-go, Agent Taylor."

Ugh. I was eager to get going, maybe too eager. Impatience had cost me in the past—just ask my parents. I wanted to talk Dom into letting me go alone, but the expression on his face took the air out of my sails.

"Nicole." Dom's voice softened, and his gaze was one of concern. "It's not just FBI regs. I don't want you in there alone. Those TSS people are heavily armed if that gun crate is any indication. They could shoot first, ask questions never."

"I get that you're worried about me." The water was up to my thighs now, and my jeans were soaking it up like a sponge. I dragged my fingertips across the surface. It was really flippin' cold, but also amazing. "Let me at least see if the way in is big enough for you. Meanwhile, you need to get your mind wrapped around getting wet."

"You better find a big, damn hole then."

I squatted down. The freezing temperature stole my breath for a moment, and I giggled. Crap. I wanted to be seen as hardcore, not giggly. I worked my hands over the grate, running my fingers from one square wire section to the next. At the bottom right, I poked my palm on a broken prong. Bingo. Weak spot.

I must have projected my excitement because Dom said, "What? What did you find?"

The lifted tine left a smallish hole about six inches wide and three inches tall. Not big enough for Dom or me, not even as a raccoon, and his bear would need something much larger. I tugged at the broken section, and it came loose in my hands. I held up the rusty tine. There was some fur, and slimy skin stuck to the end of the prong. Most likely a rodent. Yuck.

"I think I just found our way in." I threw the tine on the ground. "With a little work."

CHAPTER FOURTEEN

I dug through the soil and rocks trapping the grate in the ground and used the wire cutters on my multi-tool to cut the more rusted parts. The tool wasn't strong enough for the tines that were still in good shape. But finally, I managed to get the base free in that corner. I tried pulling up on the grate to make a hole for us, but it didn't budge. This kind of moment was the only time I wished I'd been born a bigger predator. While therianthropes were slightly stronger than humans, we did not possess superhuman strength. But the larger animals, like the coyotes, big cats, and bears, became exponentially stronger when partially shifted. Which meant...

I put the tool back in the pack and craned my neck up to look at Dom. "I'm going to need your help here."

A minute later, Dominic, with his shoes, socks, and jacket off, was knee deep in the water next to me grumbling under his breath. "Jesus, this is unpleasant."

"Ah," I shrugged, "It's not too horrible." Even though I

was in my human form, I reaped the benefits of my animal's underlayer of extra fur and fat even if it couldn't be seen.

"You're nuts," Dominic said. He shook his head. "I'm in now, so what do you want me to do?"

I took his hand. It was super warm. He had lines of calluses across his fingers. Automatically, I touched the tips. "You play guitar?"

"Yeah." He stared down at me. The pulses in his hand thudded under my touch. "Since I was eight."

"Cool." God, I sounded like a nerd. I tugged his hand into the water. "I'll guide you where the grate is the weakest. I need you to yank it free there."

"So, you only want me for my muscles."

"I've got the brains, so someone has to have the brawn," I teased.

"Can't I have both?"

"That would be unfair to the rest of the world." Oh, no. I was flirting. *Someone stop me!*

"I think the water just warmed up a degree." We submerged his hand down to his shoulder. He shivered. "Okay. Maybe not."

"There," I said. "Do you feel it?"

"I'm feeling a whole lot. Oh. Yep. There. I got it."

"Great." I let go of his hand. "Try not to make a lot of noise when you pry it up."

"Thanks for the tip." Dom's shoulder drew up and the veins in his neck bulged under the strain of his effort. He eased his muscles and closed his eyes for a moment. In seconds, his arms were covered in a fine black fur, and his shirt buttons gapped as his increased body mass stretched his clothes to their limit. He cracked his neck and stared down at me, his gray-green eyes shining with something between animal and human. In this half-form, Dominic was stunning and powerful, and that fact that he could achieve this anthropomorphic form so easily surprised me, and damn, if it didn't make me even more attracted to him.

I bit my lower lip then nodded. "Get us in, big fella."

His chest rumbled as he pulled once more on the grate. I felt the vibrations under the water as the earth gave way beneath the metal obstacle. Soon, Dom's elbows were up out of the water and debris from the other side of the culvert flowed past my legs.

"Yes!" I went up on my toes and excitement ran like a thread through me from toe to head. Impulsively, I threw my arms around Dom and kissed him. His arms wrapped around me, and I felt the hair recede on his chin and cheeks, before immediately scrambling backward, tripping over a boulder behind me, and completely submerging my whole self underwater.

Two powerful hands hauled me up. Dom's fur had receded, and so had his extra size. He gave me a weird look that I couldn't decipher, and usually, I was pretty good at reading expressions. "I think it's big enough for us to go through."

My own impulsive actions had left me unable to speak in complete sentences, or even simple words, for that matter. So I nodded and said, "Uh-huh."

"This water's not getting any warmer."

"Yep." I snapped myself out of the hormone-induced

daze. "Let's get inside." Hopefully, the preppers would still be busy with the police and the jilted Homer Halliver.

It didn't matter that I was wet from head to toe. Dom hadn't been able to get the grate high enough to prevent us from having to crawl through under water. He went first, which was a good thing, because at one point his pants snagged on the broken lattice of heavy wire, and I had to work quickly to unhook him before he drowned. Okay, maybe he wouldn't have drowned, but he did seem a little panicked when his head finally bobbed up on the other side.

I ducked down under and easily followed him through. I'd always been a good swimmer. I liked it so much, I took classes for open water diving my senior year of my undergrad. My boyfriend at the time had been advanced open water certified and had promised to take me to the Caribbean if I got mine. I did, but we broke up before he could make good on his end of the bargain. I don't know why that memory had popped up at that moment, but I shook it from my brain. I'd analyze myself later.

I swam through and came up next to Dom. I'd been in the water long enough now that the cooler temperature was starting to feel uncomfortable. "Let's get the hell on dry land."

"After last night's rainstorm, I'm not sure that's possible," Dom said. "But I know what you mean."

I regretted leaving my coat behind, but it would have just gotten soaked along with the rest of me.

The culvert didn't open up right away. There were about twenty feet of galvanized aluminum. When we reached the open end, we found ourselves on the downside of a five-foot ditch that the stream poured into. We crawled up the side and peeked our head up over the edge. In the distance, I could see red and blue cop lights flashing. We didn't hear any shouting going on, so the fight, if there had been any, was over. "Let's go before people start getting back to their posts or whatever."

"Yep," Dominic said. "On me." He scurried over the edge of the ditch and ran in a crouched position across a gravel road to the back of a nearby building.

I followed on his heels, wincing as the chunky, white gravel dug into the bottom of my feet. I missed my boots along with my coat.

The building was dark and presumably empty. Dom wiggled the door handle of the building. "Locked," he said.

With a smug expression, I grabbed my lockpick set out of the fanny pack. "See," I whispered. "It comes in handy." Using a rake, the tool that looked like a tiny comb, and a torsion wrench, I was able to pick the tumbler and unlock the door. I waggled my brows at Dom.

"Impressive," he said.

"Let's get inside." I cracked the door open and went in first. There were rows of wide metal shelves.

I pulled a large can off the nearest one. It was bulk-sized cream corn. I found dry beans, can beans, large plastic containers of flour, oats, cornmeal, powdered eggs, and powdered milk.

"Looks like we found the food pantry."

Dom nodded. "This place is stocked to last a year or

more. How long do they think this standoff with the humans is going to last?"

"I guess until they run out of grub and start eating each other."

He held up a gallon-sized container of cayenne pepper. "I bet you this would pair well with filet of human."

"Yuck." I giggled. *Stop it.* "I bet they taste like chicken."

Dominic chuckled. "Everything does."

The room was about forty feet long and probably twenty feet wide. Daylight streamed in from small windows high on the walls. We walked up and down each aisle opening items that were unmarked or unsealed. There was nothing suspicious unless you counted the entire wall of toilet paper next to a shelf full of fiber supplements. These people were serious about regularity.

"I don't think there's anything other than pantry items in here," Dom said.

"It doesn't look like it." There were six cases of paper towels stacked in front of a cabinet in the back. "Come help me with these. They might be hiding something on the lower shelves." I handed Dom the boxes one by one until they path was cleared. I sneezed. "Jesus, there is a ton of dust back here."

I peered down and stepped forward. It was mostly plastic utensils, dish soap, and industrial cleaning supplies.

"Anything?"

"Nope. I don't think anything on this shelf has been used or moved in a long time." As I inched closer, a slight breeze brushed my toes. I glanced down to see a quarter-inch crack in the floor. I stumbled trying to step over it, but the pad of my foot dropped down on the edge of the line. I heard a click. It must have been pressure activated switch because a two-foot by two-foot section of the floor dropped open beneath me. I squawked with surprise as I fell in. My leg twisted, catching on the floor as I tumbled through, falling ten feet to the cellar beneath.

"Nic!" Dom shouted. He dropped to his stomach and peered down at me. "Nic! Are you okay?"

"I should have stepped over the crack," I groaned. Was it the prophecy again? Were Sunny's predictions coming true? I didn't want to believe it, but so far, she was two for two.

"Are you hurt?"

I tried to stand up, but the excruciating pain in my right foot, ankle, and calf made it impossible. "I think I broke my ankle. Or at least, sprained it pretty bad."

"I'm coming down. Crawl back, so I don't land on you."

I scooted back using my arms and my good foot to push me. My fingers brushed over something rough, thin, and small. Dom dropped down, and with only the trickle of moonlight through the trap door, it was impossible to see much in the dank cellar, but now that my adrenaline waned and my pain receptors kicked into high gear, I could smell a sweetly scented rot in the room.

I pulled my LED thumb light from my fanny pack and turned it on. The smell in the room resembled a kill room at a chicken factory. Foul. No pun intended. "Dom, something has died down here."

"Animal or human," he asked as he knelt next to me.

He scooped me up into his arms, cradling me against his body.

"You tell me." A bear's olfactory senses were sharper than a raccoon's.

"With that much decay, it's hard to tell. It's probably coming up from the drain. This may be where they butcher their meat in the winter."

I swung the light around the room. I could see a water spigot on the wall near me, and a drain trap in the center of the floor, but the light wasn't powerful enough to get a good view of the entire place. I put the light on the object I'd discovered. It was plastic and chewed at the end.

"Hey, I think this belonged to Lloyd Evan. Remember? The other night he took one of those plastic toothpicks from his pocket and was chewing on it like it was a last meal."

"Could be. Put it in that fanny pack of yours. We'll see if we can test for DNA."

Luckily, I had some tiny snack sized baggies. I stuck the pick in one and the piece of metal in another. "We need to get out of here before someone shows up, and I don't see a door or a ladder."

"Yeah, that's suspect. We can't worry about it now. You're hurt, and the longer we stay down here, the more likely we're going to get caught. We'll come in here tomorrow with the warrant and accidentally find the trap door."

"I want to do one quick sweep of the room first. This light's not very good, and maybe we're missing something. Besides, the smell, while gross, is fresher than that dust up there. There has to be another way in here because those boxes above haven't been moved in a very long time."

Dom cupped my cheek. "Okay, we'll walk around once. If we don't trip over anything or find any secret passage, we're out."

I pressed my palm against the back of his hand. "Agreed."

As he walked the floor, we both heard a sound like plastic dropping on the concrete. "I kicked something," he said. Dom squatted while still holding me, which I found super impressive but when he stood up, he smacked my hurt ankle against the wall.

"Ow, ow, ow."

"Sorry, sorry," he said with real sincerity. "It's a broken piece of metal or something. It's got a pattern cut into the top, and it feels rough and damaged."

"Pocket it." I swung the light at the walls. In the back, there was a black sheet hanging across the wall. I had "T.S.S." sewn on in white letters, and under that, it said, "Freedom isn't free."

"What's that?" I squiggled the light over the signage.

"Let's check it out."

He walked us over, and we pulled back the sheet. A large metal door with several bolts and slide locks, all of them engaged, was set in the wall. "There's our out if we can get the door unlocked."

"Or it could lead us right into the hands of the TSS. We don't know that it goes outside the compound."

My eyes watered as the pain in my foot worsened. I

flinched but didn't complain. "There is only one way to find out."

"But if we go this way, the preppers will know we've been here. We have to close the trap door and put the boxes back. We can search it tomorrow when we come back with the warrant. Besides, you need to see the doctor."

I wanted to argue, but the pain was excruciating now. I nodded. "Fine. Let's go. I think I'm going to have to shift or there's no way we're getting out of here unnoticed. My raccoon form can function better with a hurt ankle."

"When you shift back you'll be naked." He didn't sound disappointed.

"Yeah, but you won't see it because I'm not shifting back until you get me to Doctor Smith's place."

I could hear the grin in Dom's voice. "Spoilsport."

"Yep. Now let's get out of here."

Dom lifted me until I could grab the edge of the upper floor and pull myself into the pantry. When I was all the way through, I looked down at him and shined the light in his eyes. The pain increased, so my next words were through gritted teeth. "Give me thirty seconds then come up here and grab my clothes."

"You really are a spoilsport," Dom teased.

I hurt too bad to laugh. "You might have to carry me to the stream, but at least I'll be small enough that I won't slow you down." Tears leaked down the side of my face.

"I'd already planned on it, Nic," Dom said. "You just get yourself ready. I'll be up in thirty seconds.

I stripped as fast as the agony would allow, closed my

eyes and pushed my beast forward. She eagerly climbed forward as fur sprout over my body and bushed out in bands of white, gray, and black. The magic that came with being a therianthrope made shifting pleasurable, and it had been too long since I'd changed without the full moon. I forgot how wonderful it felt to be in this clever, little body. I wiggled my paws, and while my foot and ankle still hurt, the pain has lessened. I tried to walk forward, but my foot dragged. Luckily, before I could do more damage, Dom scooped me up again.

"I got you, darling," he said, holding me close. "I got you."

CHAPTER FIFTEEN

*D*om had carried me to the car then went back for our coats and shoes. My foot and ankle throbbed like crazy. It was worse than the time I'd stepped into a hole playing right field in a class softball game. I'd been the smallest person in my sixth-grade class, so the appointed team captain had stuck me in the position with the least amount of responsibility. Eldin had helped me off the field that day, and we'd become fast friends.

That's when I'd developed a crush on him. He'd been my hero. I curled in a ball, careful of my foot, and glanced up at my determined partner as we drove us down the road. He caught my gaze and put his hand down on my head and stroked my neck.

"It's going to be okay, Nic."

He petted me. I wanted to be taken aback, but the gesture was sweet. Tender even. The only therian boyfriend I'd ever had was Eldin. In college, I'd only dated humans. It's not like we could take out ads saying, "single shifter looking for same." It was both strange and wondrous having someone touch me while I was in my animal body. I rubbed my cheek against the back of his hand.

He smiled but kept his eyes on the road. "We're almost there. Just passed the bridge out of town." His fingers trailed down my back. Instinctually, I licked his forearm then quickly moved my head back mortified I'd just tried to clean my partner, something raccoons did when being affectionate.

I waited for the teasing I knew would follow, but he just kept stroking my fur with one hand while gripping the wheel with the other. "Pulling into the drive now."

When he brought the car to a stop, he scrambled out, and I could hear him pounding on the doc's door. He didn't stop until I heard a woman say, "I heard you! What's is going on, Dom?"

It was Chavvah.

"We need to see Billy Bob. Nicole's hurt."

The next few minutes passed quickly as Dom took me from the car and carried me through the Doc's house down a long hallway to the door that led into the clinic. He gently put me down on a patient bed in one of the rooms.

Doctor Smith curled his finger under my chin and smiled. "We'll give you a minute to change."

Suddenly, I didn't want Dominic to leave. My reasoning side didn't want to be naked and vulnerable in front of him, but my raccoon side found him comforting. He made me feel safe. I reached out with my paws and gripped Dom's finger. He looked down at me, a question in his eyes.

"I'll be right outside the door," he said.

I gripped his finger tighter.

The hard worry lines at the corners of his eyes soft-ened. "You don't want me to leave?" I willed my fingers to open and let him go, but those crazy kids had a mind of their own. Dom looked at Doctor Smith. "I guess I'm staying."

"If Nic is okay with you being in here then I don't mind. I'll be back in a few minutes." Doctor Smith exited the room. Only then did I let Dom's finger go.

I rotated on the bed and shoved my nose under the white sheet and light coral colored blanket. Dominic helped by lifting up the edge so I could crawl under. When I got myself completely under and turned around, I closed my eyes and willed the shift from animal to human. It didn't feel as good as turning into a raccoon, but it wasn't unpleasant. I forgot, though, the slight disappoint-ment I always felt when I would lose the heightened sense of touch, smell, and sight. My biped form was better than a regular human, but nowhere near as in tune as my animal. It wasn't the same as being forced to shift on the first full moon every month. That involuntary shifting produced an animal that acted on pure instinct, and for the past nine years, I hadn't allowed myself to shift at any other time.

Now that I had, I realized how much I missed it. It was the reason many therianthropes staying in closed commu-nities. It was a freedom to be who we are without worrying about humans trying to kill or trap us. My animal counter-part was hunted for sport regularly in the Midwest. I can remember my father's warnings about leaving our woods. For a moment, I understood the fears of the TSS.

Dom's warm fingers touched my cheek, and he wiped a tear that had spilled down it. "You're in pain. I'll go get the doc."

I was in pain, now that I was back in my frailer body, but that wasn't why I cried. I grabbed Dominic's hand again.

His brow lowered. "What's wrong?"

I cleared my throat, my voice a little raspy from the transformation. "Thanks." I scooched up the bed while holding the covers to my chest. "Ah!" I winced as my injured ankle turned.

Dom untucked the covers at the bottom and lifted them over my foot to free it. "Ouch," he said. "That looks angry."

My ankle was red and swollen to the size of a navel orange. "It feels angry." Though not as much as it had before shifting. Therianthropes healed quicker than humans, but it was nothing like what people wrote about in fiction or in the movies. Not even turning would speed up the process.

Dom sat on the side of the bed, his hip pressed up against mine. "I don't like you being hurt."

I grimaced. "I don't like it much either."

He took my hand in between both of his. "No," he said. "I really don't like seeing your hurt. I know it's just an ankle, but damn, Nic. I wanted to run all the way here to get you fixed. I had to fight myself just to go back for the stuff we'd left by the culvert. You mess my head up."

I blushed. "I bet you say that to all the girls."

"I've never said that to another woman, darling."

Goose bumps raised on my arms as a flush crept into my cheeks. I remembered him calling me darling when he'd carried me to the car. I'd mortified myself by snuggling against his chest, taking comfort in his heat. "Stop," I said quietly. "Don't lie to me."

He leaned down and kissed my forehead. When I didn't move away, he kissed my lips. Soft and sweet. "I'll never lie to you."

My mouth parted as a myriad of declarations prepared to pour out. *Knock, knock, knock.* I closed my mouth.

Dominic gave me a lopsided grin. "Saved by the doctor."

"No kidding," I said with feelings of relief and disappointment.

"You ready?" asked Doctor Smith through the door.

"Yep," I said loud enough for him to hear. I met Dom's gaze as he took my hand. I nodded. "I'm ready."

A COUPLE OF HOURS AND an X-ray later, I was at my parents' home in the living room with my wrapped foot propped up on the couch. There was no break, just a bad sprain. Doc had given me some pain meds and wrapped my ankle up. He'd also given me a splint to wear that would fit in my shoe, but told me to keep off the foot for a day or two. But, as I told Dominic on the way to my folks', there was no way in hell I was missing the search in the morning.

"So, how did you twist your ankle again?" My dad asked.

I had come up with a story about me tripping up a step, but it made my gut hurt to try and say it out loud. I looked at Dominic, imploring him to be the liar, liar, pants on fire. He nodded.

"We snuck onto the TSS compound earlier, and Nic fell down through a trap door in their food pantry," Dom said.

Dad's eyes widened, my eyes widened, Mom gasped as she brought a bag of ice in from the kitchen, and Dom shrugged. I guess I wasn't the only one uncomfortable with lying to Dad.

"What in the Sam Hill is he talking about, Nicole Rae?"

I groaned. When Dad used my first and middle name, it was almost worse than him calling me Puddin.

He turned to my dad. "We were in and out before anyone saw us, and the room under the pantry is pretty suspicious."

"Yep," I agreed. "It smelled like rotting meat down there."

"And we found this," Dom said. He held up the metal piece we'd found on the floor in the cellar. "Maybe a hairpin or something." He handed it to my dad. "The end has been scraped and worn."

My dad held the object up and examined it from all sides. Finally, he handed it back. "So, for all your trouble, all you got was a piece of trash someone dropped."

"We also found a chewed-up plastic toothpick," I said in our defense since Dom was no help at all. "Doctor Smith is going to help us get DNA to see if it matches any of our victims, including Lloyd Evans." I let my shoulders fall, and my head slumped forward a little. "Of course, he said the test will probably take a couple of weeks, even with a rush put on them. However, he did say he might be able to match the marks with Evans' teeth if it's his."

"And then what?" My dad clenched and unclenched his fists. "You two are the two biggest dumbasses on the planet." Dad's tone simmered with anger. "You contaminated a potential crime scene. Walked out with evidence that we can no longer connect to the place." He waved his hand. "I can't talk about this anymore with you. Judge Holt and his wife are coming by for dinner tonight. He's bringing the warrant I dropped off at the courthouse today. You two keep your mouths shut about your little illegal adventure."

I wanted to be indignant, but chances were good he was right about the piece of metal being trash and us being dumbasses, though I didn't think there was any way we were the biggest on earth. "Dad..."

He held up his hand. "I should haul both of your asses into jail for breaking and entering, criminal trespass, and a half a dozen more charges I'll think of on the way to the station."

"But you won't," I said hopefully.

My Dad's penetrating gaze made me squirm. "No. I won't." He walked around the back of the couch and put his hand on my head. "I'm really mad at you right now, Nicole." With a quick pat, he strolled down the hall to his home office, the room right before the guest bedroom.

My mom shook her head at me. "That man adores you, Nicole. You need to stop lying to him."

"I know, Mom. I'm sorry." God, I was gutted. The look on my dad's face when he'd walked away had reflected the displeasure I saw in my mom's expression.

"I'm not the one you need to apologize to." She placed the ice pack on my ankle. "Don't take too long to think about it." And with that final admonishment, Mom went back to the kitchen, leaving Dom and me alone.

He pursed his lips in a frown. "Sorry." He drew his shoulders up in a partial shrug.

"You left me looking like the jerk." I pointed at him. "Why the hell didn't you tell him the stair story?"

"Why didn't you?"

Because I was a coward, who didn't want to lie to my dad. And now I felt like an asshole for asking Dom to take the heat I deserved. Maybe my parents treated me like I was 12 years old because I was acting like it.

"Look, Nic, I couldn't bring myself to lie to him," Dom said, clear exasperation in his voice. "I freaking like you, okay? I don't want to get on the wrong foot with your father."

"Too late for that. You and I are in the same boat on shit's creek."

"I'm not talking about parental ire."

"I know. We...we can't," I told him half-heartedly. "We are partners. It's against the FBI policy on fraternization."

Dom knelt down next to me. "We've already broken a dozen rules. What's one more?" He cupped my chin and kissed me. A zing of exhilaration zipped through me as his tongue wet my parted lips. I leaned into the kiss, my hands encircling his neck as I opened for him, inviting the invasion. Dom moaned as his large arm wrapped around my waist, and he pulled my chest against his. God, his body temperature warmed me to the bone.

And speaking of bone, my hip brushed against his groin, and the thick bulge was hard as a rock. I squirmed, only hurting my ankle twice, as I maneuvered to wrap my legs around his waist.

"Nicole. Rae. Taylor," snapped my mother.

I yelped as I pushed Dominic away from me and his body hit my foot. I swung my feet back up on the couch and put the ice pack on my injury and pretended my mom had not just walked in on my trying to dry hump my partner.

Dom looked dazed like the cat seduced by the canary.

"Look here, Smokey and the Bandit." Mom snapped her fingers. "The Judge and Judy are going to be here any minute. You need to stop acting like two lovesick teenagers who have discovered their bodies for the first time."

My cheeks flamed. "Mom!"

"My apologies, Mrs. Taylor," Dom said.

I glared at him.

I was beginning to think he needed to worry a lot less about what my parents thought of him and more about the fact that I was going to kill him.

CHAPTER SIXTEEN

*I*t was already seven o'clock, and with Mom's help, and at her insistence, I'd managed to get changed into a midnight blue blouse with a deeper vee than Mom liked, but it was one of my favorite shirts, and a pair black palazzo pants that were easy to get over my splinted ankle without causing any more damage. I wore my black tennis shoes tied loose on the right foot. The palazzo pants were wide enough to hide them.

Mom also helped me with my hair, and by help, I mean she broke out the curling iron and her industrial size canister of hairspray. I hadn't taken a curling iron to my hair since I'd set out for college. I had to put my foot down when she came at me with foundation and a makeup sponge, though I did acquiesce and put on a little blush, pale pink eyeshadow, and some rose-tinted lip gloss.

"Good enough?" I asked.

Mom looked me over, my foot elevated once again on the end of the couch. Her brow furrowed and she frowned. "You'll do. The Holts will be here any minute. I hope your dad has at least changed his shirt."

My dad hadn't come out of his office since he'd stormed out of the living room, and Dom had gone to shower, dress, and make a few phone calls.

Mom sat down on the couch next to me. "You and Agent Tartan, huh?"

"I don't know what you mean."

"I haven't had a sudden case of amnesia, little girl. It wasn't an hour ago, I walked in on the two you making out on this very couch."

"You know, Mom, short-term memory is often the first thing to go as you get old and infirmed."

"You're awfully cheeky, girl. I'll have you know that I am in the prime of my life." Her lips upturned in a sly smile. "Your father has no complaints."

"Ewwww! Mom. Yuck. Yuck. Where do you keep the brain bleach?"

Mom laughed. "Serves you right." He brushed my hair back from my face. "You're such a pretty girl, Nicole."

"Stop it now."

"And even if you can't see it, that boy in the other room is smitten with you."

"What is this? The nineteen-hundreds?"

Mom gave me a quick backhand to my shoulder.

I laughed. "Child abuse!"

"I'm going to put you in an orphanage."

"And I'm going to put you in a home." It was an age-old banter between us.

She laughed. "I love you, Puddin'. It's nice to have you home."

"I love you back," I said.

She kissed my cheek. "I'll stop grilling you about Dominic, but only because I have to get the roast out of the oven and finish the mashed potatoes."

"Dom!" I yelled since it was more expedient than walking. "Can you bring me the files? I want to look at them to see if we missed something. Or if something old clicks as something new."

"Just a minute," he bellowed from the guest room. A few minutes later, he came into the living room. "Here you go. Sorry, I was on the phone with Resnik."

"Anything new out of Springfield?"

"No. Lieberman's wife has been calling Resnik for updates. She's understandably upset," he said. "I have her number. I'm going to give her a call in a little bit."

"But we don't know anything new." I took the files from him. "Damn it. Why don't we have anything new?"

"It's the job," Dom said. "Only messy killers get caught fast. Our guy isn't messy."

"Except this time. I don't understand why he's different than the other victims. Why keep him this long?"

"That's the question, isn't it? Maybe talking to the wife, asking her some questions about their life, his work, his personalities, and habits, is the way to go. We know what he has in common with the other victims, maybe it's time to look at the variances."

"The other three victims, two were married, the other

in the process of divorcing. Maybe we should speak to their wives as well."

"It's going to stir up old wounds."

I sighed. "I know, but I don't think it can be helped."

"The second victim's wife is human. She's unaware of his therianthrope status."

"He was a deer shifter, right?"

"That's right. The first victim was an opossum and the third, a raccoon."

"All non-predators," I noted.

"Do you think that has something to do with how he chooses his victims?"

"Maybe. But it's likely they were just the most readily available victims."

Dom gave me a questioning look. "Elaborate."

"It's not a coincidence that the non-predator therians are more likely to integrate. They don't have to worry about hurting humans on a full moon. There has never been a single report of a human being killed by an attack squirrel."

Dom chuckled. "True."

"On top of that, being a non-predator in a community half full of predators can sometimes get you walked on."

"That doesn't seem to be a problem in Peculiar."

"That's because we have a nice blend of therians. People can overcome their instincts to dominate if they try hard. Even so, there can still be some bullying that happens."

Dom put his hand over mine and gave it a gentle squeeze. "Is that why you decided to integrate?"

I turned my palm into his. "Nothing that dramatic."

The doorbell chimed. I raised my brows. "That's the judge and his wife, Judy."

"Judge Judy," Dom said. "Isn't that a daytime TV series?"

"Try not to embarrass me in front of the Holts." I giggled. Damn it. I'd giggled more in the past three days than I had in years. "No Judge Judy comments."

He drew a cross with his finger over his chest. "Cross my heart."

My heart quickened. God, this man gave me palpitations.

"You look faint. Are you feeling well?"

"Fine." I had a disease called lust, and there was no cure in sight.

"Sid," my mom called loudly. "Company's here!"

My dad, who had been in hiding since our breaking and entering revelation, stalked down the hallway, his shoulders tight and his hands in balled fists at his sides. When the judge and his wife rounded the corner with mom, Dad visibly relaxed. He put on a friendly smile, and said, "Hey, Harry, good to see you." He leaned over and brushed Judy's cheek with his lips. "You're looking lovely," he told her.

"You've always been such a charmer, Sid." She smiled at my mother. "You're a lucky woman, Jean."

"I'd say we both hit the lottery," Mom replied politely. "Judge. Judy." Mom pointed to Dom and me. I had to elbow Dom when he chuckled. "You know my daughter Nicole and her work partner, Dominic Tartan."

"Nicole," Judy said. "Aren't you a pretty little thing? I hear you some big degree from an Ivy League school."

"Yep," I said. I hated being referred to as a "pretty little thing" like I was some kind of bauble or a piece of jewelry, not a person. I wanted to say, pretty little thing my ass, you best call me Doctor Taylor. But my parents would die of shame on the spot.

"It's nice to meet you, ma'am," Dom said. He gave her hand a quick shake. I didn't like the way she eyeballed his backside when Dom turned to the judge and shook his hand next. "Good to see you, Judge."

"Agent Tartan." The judge held on for an extra second. "Any new leads on the case?"

"Afraid not, but we appreciate you being quick with the warrants."

"I'm happy to help."

"I'm sorry if it's causing problems with your family," I said. "I know you have some kin still behind the walls."

"My parents were die-hard believers in the TSS. I'm afraid I never feared humans as much as they did."

My dad poured himself, Dominic, and the judge a whiskey. "Harry's dad was one of the original five founders."

"Wow, a legacy," I said.

"Yes," the judge said, taking a sip of the bourbon. "But dad died when I was ten. My mom stayed with the TSS, but I left when I turned eighteen. Headed off to college and learned the law. At first, I wanted to be able to help our kind by finding ways to fight inside the system, but after living among the humans in plain sight for seven years, I just stopped being afraid. I think a lot of them would if they could get past their fears and stop walling off the world."

I looked at the judge, reevaluating my opinion of him. I'd always thought he was fair, but I hadn't realized how far he'd had to come. "That's very progressive of you, Judge Holt. I'm impressed. Is your mom still living out there?"

His smile faded. "She passed a couple of years back. Lung cancer."

"I'm sorry for your loss."

His eyes brightened. "Let's talk about less unpleasant things." He sniffed the air. "Like that delicious pot roast I smell."

My mom clapped her hands together. "And luckily, it's ready now." She looked at Dom. "Dominic, will you help our Nicole to the table?"

I gave Mom a sharp look, but she'd already turned on her heel toward the dining room.

"You heard your Mom. I'm to help *our* Nicole to the table."

"I'm my own...oh, never mind. Could you hand me the crutches? I can hobble myself in."

"Nothing doing. Your mom gave me a job to do it, and I'm doing it." He reached his arms around me and lifted me in the air.

"I am not a rag doll to be carried around," I protested as he cradled me in his arms. "Besides, my foot feels a lot better. So, put me down."

"Fine." He set me down on my good foot. "You can put your arm around me for support."

"Fine," I said back. I hopped into the dining room with my arm around Dominic's waist. His muscles shifted and flexed under my hand. His arm crossed my upper back, and his hand was under my armpit. His fingers brushed the top of my ribs, and I inhaled a quick breath.

"I'm not going to be able to concentrate on food if you keep that up," I said in a bare whisper.

"Happy accident," Dom said with a wicked glint in his eye.

He escorted me into the dining room. My dad sat at the head of my family's hand-carved golden oak dining table. It seated six normally, eight with the leaf in. Mom wanted to appear grand, so she'd put the leaf in and added some candle centerpieces encircled with purple, green, and gold silk flowers. My dad sat at the head of the table and my mom to his right. Judge Holt sat at the other end, his wife to the right of him. Dom sat me next to Mom, and he took the seat next to Judy.

"What did you do to your foot, Nicole?" the judge asked.

"I tripped up the stairs," I said with our original lie. I gave a Dom a look that said, "See, that's how you do it."

"That's bad luck," Judy said. "I hope you didn't break anything."

"Doc says it's just a sprain. I've always been a little clumsy."

Dominic laughed. "The first time I met her she tripped right into my arms."

"What a wonderful meet-cute," Judy said.

"I have no idea what that means," my mom said.

155

I'd heard the term before, and it made me barf in my mouth a little. I would not have my relationship with Dom reduced to something called a meet-cute.

Judy happily explained though. "It's when a man and woman meet in a cute way and are destined to be together."

I sighed. "We are work colleagues."

Judy reached down, and it looked like she put her hand on Dominic's thigh. "That's how it always starts, lovey." She cast a casual glance at her husband. "Harry and I met when he first started his practice. I was a legal secretary at the firm. I'd been an integrator my whole life, but when I met him, I knew I'd follow him anywhere." She laughed. "Even to the middle of nowhere!" Her hand never came back up to the table.

Outwardly, I politely chuckled, but inwardly I was rolling my eyes, groaning, and flipping her the bird while vehemently threatening her within an inch of her life if she didn't get her hand off Dominic's leg. His eyes widened at me. It was the first time I'd seen anything resembling fear in his expression.

"Uhm, oh, shoot," I said feigning disappointment. "I forgot that Dom and I were supposed to meet Eldin Farraday for dinner. All the excitement this afternoon, between the trip and the doctor's clinic, I forgot all about it."

"You can call him and cancel," Mom insisted.

I looked a Dom for support. If that bastard took Mom's side, I was going to neuter him. He put down his napkin and slid back from the table. Judy's hand went up and to her chest, surprised by his abrupt movement. "Yep, I forgot. He said he has some things about the case he wanted to discuss."

"Oh, yeah," my dad said. "Why didn't my own deputy say anything to me?"

"You know, Dad, he has a few theories he wanted to discuss. Pure speculation." I stood up and started hobbling toward the door. "Got to go. Come on, Dom. We're already late." I grabbed my crutches by the coat rack.

"Let me help," Dom said, grabbing my coat.

I snatched it from him. "No time."

When we exited the front door, closing it behind us, we both started laughing. Dom put his arm around me. "So, what are we really doing?"

"Going to Eldin's."

"Why?"

"Because my parents will check and I can't get caught in an actual lie."

Dom nodded, but not like he was happy about it. "Then I guess we go to Farraday's."

"Eldin is a really nice guy and one of my oldest friends. I wish you'd be a little nicer to him."

Dom opened the passenger door. I slid my crutches into the back seat and dropped into the seat backward and lifted my legs inside the car.

After he shut the door, I heard him say, "I wish he were a little less nice to you."

CHAPTER SEVENTEEN

I'd texted Eldin to make sure he was home because he wouldn't lie to my father for any reason, and I couldn't take it if my dad looked at me again the way he had earlier. It would be too painful. Almost like this car ride had been. Dom had been curiously silent as I gave him directions to Eldin's place.

"If you take this next right, he the second house on the right." I pointed to Summit Street. "He lives in his parents' place."

"With his parents?"

"No. They moved to a small place outside of town and gave Eldin the house. I think they were trying to distance themselves from Peculiar after the whole thing with Neville Lutjen selling our kind to hunters for big sport."

"I was read in on the council's report."

"By Willy?" I asked.

Dom grimaced. "Yep."

"What happened between you two? Did you break her

heart?" I glanced at him to read his expression. It was blank, but his knuckles were white as he gripped the steering wheel to make the turn.

"I thought I loved her. She didn't think she loved me. She was the wild girl everyone wanted to tame."

Was that his type? The wild girl. If so, there was no way I'd keep his interest. "I'm not a wild girl," I said.

"Good."

"Oh, I get it," I said. "She hurt you, so you are determined to date her opposite. I'm no one's consolation prize. This thing between us isn't going to work if your only interest in me is that I'm not her."

Dom slammed on the brakes out front of Eldin's house. "My interest in you has nothing to do with Willy Boden."

"I don't believe you."

He turned in his seat, gripped my shoulders, and kissed me completely breathless.

"That's not an answer," I said airily. My pulse thudded in my throat and much lower parts of my anatomy.

"Isn't it?" He stroked my cheek. "I told you that I'd thought I loved her. It's only been this week that I realized what I felt for Willy was trivial, it was nothing, a brief infatuation. I've never had a woman make me feel like you make me feel."

"And how's that?"

"Excited, protective, frustrated, worried, hopeful."

"Anything else?"

"Scared."

"Scared?"

"Scared that I'll lose you. I don't want to be without you, Nic."

"We haven't known each other but a few days."

"I know you have feelings for me. What's holding you back?" He raised his brows. "Eldin Farraday? Are you in love with him?"

A knock on the window had us both jumping to our respective sides of the car.

Eldin's face pressed against the glass. "Nicole? Agent Tartan? What are you all doing out here?"

I met Dom's gaze. "Setting the record straight," I said. "I'm not in love with Eldin."

Dominic's chiseled features softened. "Okay."

Eldin, who looked even more confused, said, "Good to know. Why don't you park this sedan and come on in? I have cold beer in the fridge. I think we're all going to need it."

Dom parked the car and raced around to the passenger side to help me out. He got my crutches, and, even though I hated being babied, the way he hovered over me was actually sort of sweet. Eldin held to door open as I swung my feet inside. As we made our way into the living room, I saw a man in jeans and a vee-neck forest green sweater sitting on the couch with a bottle of beer in hand. "Deputy Thompson?" I asked.

"Nope, wrong brother," the guy said, standing up. Now I could see, while he looked almost identical to Tyler Thompson, this man was a bit thinner, more muscular. This was Taylor Thompson.

Eldin went and stood beside him, "Nic, I have been

trying to tell you something ever since I saw you in Springfield."

"You have?" I blinked because I hadn't noticed. Had I really been so self-absorbed?

"I'm just going to say it quick. Like a bandage ripped off a wound."

Taylor gave Eldin a sour look. "I'm not a wound."

"I didn't mean it like that." Anyhow. He flexed his fingers. "Nicole. This is Taylor Thompson."

I nodded. "I'm aware."

"My boyfriend."

"I'm..." Clueless? Blind? Stymied? Oblivious? Jesus H. Christ and the whole choir of angels, I had been completely obtuse. "How long have you...?" It was a dumb question. I was a freaking shrink. I knew sexuality didn't just happen magically out of the blue. Eldin Farraday was gay. And he'd been gay his whole life. "But we..." I was handling this soooo badly. "But you...God, Eldin. You broke my heart our senior year."

"Please don't be mad at me," he said. His fingers laced with Taylor's.

"I'm not mad," I said. I had a gazillion feelings going on. Anger wasn't one of them. "I'm a little hurt that you didn't trust me enough to tell me, but I'm not mad." I did what I should have done when he first announced he had a boyfriend, I limped forward and threw my arms around his neck. "Are you happy?"

"Yes," Eldin said. "I'm very happy."

"Then I'm happy for you."

He must have dropped Taylor's hand because both his

arms went around me. "You know, Nic, you're the only girl I ever loved. I'm sorry I couldn't be what you needed."

I cast a quick glance over my shoulder at Dom, who, for the record, was grinning like a fool. "Don't be sorry. I'm not. Not at all." I jumped back on one foot and used Dom's forearm to steady me. "So," I asked, "how many people know?"

Taylor took the lead. "My family knows. And if my mom knows something, everyone in earshot knows."

I laughed. "Ruth still makes the best pies in town."

"There's one in the fridge I can heat up if you'd like."

I fist pumped my arm. "If you have some vanilla ice cream the answer is yes, yes, yes. Oh, hell, even if you don't have ice cream, I will definitely take the warm pie."

Eldin and Dom helped me to the couch when Taylor ducked into the kitchen. I turned to my high school sweetheart and took his hand. "How did I miss the signs?"

"I'm very macho," Eldin said. His narrow features and high cheekbones always made him look a little elfish. Manly, yes. Macho, not so much. We both chuckled. "I'm terrible at this profiling thing."

"So, tell me about your ankle. What happened?"

"Can Taylor keep a secret or will he tell Deputy Thompson?"

"My identical twin didn't find out I was gay until I told him on our twentieth birthday," Taylor said from the other room. "I'm awesome with secrets."

We laid out the entire afternoon for Eldin and Taylor over some of the most magnificent blueberry pie I'd ever eaten. "You mom should box this crust and sell it as magic. She would make a million dollars."

"I'll tell her you said so. It'll make her feel good," the blond deer shifter said.

Eldin leaned forward. "So, you guys found a hidden cellar through a dusty trap door with a secret entrance underground? That's some *Silence of the Lambs'* shit there. Do you think this has anything to do with your case? Or just Lloyd's murder? Or the guns?"

"Maybe all three. We don't know. We have to find out where that door leads, though." Dom said.

I nodded. "My gut is telling me that tomorrow will be too late."

Eldin tilted his head at me. "It's now or never."

"Do not break out in song," I told him.

He laughed. "You know you love my Elvis impersonation."

Taylor snapped his fingers. "Hey. Some old bomb shelters and tunnels had been built—back in the late fifties when people were worried about atomic warfare. I'm pretty sure I could get into the zoning office and find some of the old property maps for that area."

Eldin hugged Taylor to him. "You're brilliant, babe." He turned to me. "Taylor is the human resource manager at City Hall. He does all the hiring and managing of the non-elected positions."

"I have the master key, so I can get into any room I want."

I looked at Dom, and I could see his excitement level had kicked up a notch. "I'm in."

"This is some real James Bond shit," Taylor said.

Eldin grinned. "Sean Connery?"

"Who else?" Taylor stood up and gave Eldin a hand up. In a fairly good imitation of the original, he said in a spot on Scottish accent, "Shall we go, Money Penny?"

Dom helped me to my feet next. In my ear, he said, "I can't believe I was worried about this dork."

I giggled. "Come on, double-o-nerds. We have a City Hall to break into."

Taylor shook his head. "It's not breaking if you have the keys."

"I like you, Taylor Thompson."

"Thank heavens, because I think Eldin would have dumped me if you didn't approve."

At least three of us walked out of Eldin's house humming the theme song for Mission Impossible.

When we got into the car, Dom's eyes were bright. Happy. "Thanks for rescuing me from Judy at dinner. That woman is grabby."

I wrinkled my nose at him. "It was either rescue you or come flying across the pot roast to snatch her hair extensions form her head. I did not like that woman touching you."

"Really?"

"I was already thinking about places to bury the body."

Dom's grin grew ridiculously wide. "I've had Eldin buried several times since he met us in Springfield."

"We're a pair," I said as Dom started the engine and followed Taylor and Eldin in Taylor's car.

"We sure are, partner."

CHAPTER EIGHTEEN

*D*om carried me piggy-back style into City Hall and down two sets of stairs to the basement. The county assessor had moved all the old deeds and property assessments along with maps to a large storage room off the main entrance.

Taylor put his key in the door and jiggled it. It wouldn't turn.

"I left my lockpicks at home, so I hope you can get this open."

Dom turned his head over his shoulder and said to me, "I can't believe we forgot to bring the fanny pack."

"In our defense, I wasn't planning to *not*-break and enter into City Hall."

Dom, with his forearms under my knees, hoisted me up higher on his back. "In my defense," he emphasized the word my, "I think you're a bad influence on me."

Eldin snickered. "He knows you so well, Nic." He

looked at Dom. "I was a model student and citizen until I started hanging out with Nicole."

I squeezed my thighs against Dom and pointed indignantly at Eldin. "You were thirteen-years-old. You weren't even fully formed yet when I found you. You cannot blame me for your bad behavior."

"Sure I can," he said. "I do it all the time."

"Still?"

"Got it!" Taylor said. He opened the door. "And to answer your question, yes, Eldin blames you all the time." He winked at me and gestured for all us to enter.

"Are there any guards who patrol here at night?" Dom asked when Taylor turned on the light in the room.

"This is Peculiar, not some metropolis, and besides, this room has no windows, not even in the door, so," he closed the door, "no one is going to see the light on."

We searched for only half an hour before Eldin said, "Bingo!"

"How's your back holding up?" I asked Dom. He hadn't put me down once since we'd exited the car.

"It's fine." He raised me up again.

"You can put me down if I'm getting too heavy."

"I've carried weapons and rucksacks heavier than you."

"Rucksacks?"

"I was Army Intelligence before I joined the FBI."

"How freaking old are you?"

"Old enough to know better, but young enough to do it anyway."

"Will you two stop flirting and get over here?" Eldin

took a stack of rolled-up papers out of a cylindrical canister. "I've got the maps."

I looked over Dominic's shoulder at the property description and the topographical outlines. There were several areas that crossed. "There," I said, indicating the stream we knew flowed under the gate. "Right there where the stream comes in from the right, that where we breached the compound. We probably went about twenty to thirty feet before we crawled out of the creek bed, across a road to a building probably the same distance. So go back another twenty feet and to the right about ten feet and that's where we saw the underground door."

Dom poked his finger on the map. "And there's the tunnel. The description says a storm shelter was built in this location. They must have built the pantry over the top of it."

"There was so much dust, I can't imagine more than a few people still know the underground room exists."

"Well," Taylor said, "if this map is accurate, it looks like the tunnel comes out over here." He indicated a spot near the edge of the property that bordered a big pond.

"That's probably where the stream empties."

Eldin nodded. "You know, that pond is at the edge of Brady Corman's new property. He is building a house out there for Willy and their new babies."

"Those kids are going to have the biggest potty mouths," Taylor said.

Dom laughed. "That's the God's honest truth. That woman can make the people who make sailors blush blush."

"I'm sure Deputy Boden will be a fine mother." I rested my upper arms on Dom's shoulders and rubbed my hands together. "Let's go find ourselves a super-secret entrance to this evil lair."

TAYLOR THOMPSON HAD been an immediate, hellz yes, but Dom and Eldin had taken some coercing. Dom would learn soon enough that I was a girl who liked to get her way. Eldin already knew that about me, which is why I couldn't understand what took him so long to get on board...until I realized he was worried something might happen to Taylor, the only civilian in the bunch.

However, Taylor, in no uncertain terms, told Eldin he was going with or without him. I'd given the same speech to Dom, and both men reluctantly agreed to join us on this little adventure.

Mr. Corman hadn't finished the house yet, so the property was vacant. Good. I didn't want to have to beg Willy for any favors. I mean, I liked the woman, she was feisty as hell, but I didn't really want to hang out with Dominic's ex-girlfriend if I could help it.

Since I wasn't about to go home to grab my gear, we had to make due with what Eldin had laying around his house. Two small flashlights, some pore tweezers and a pore remover that I hoped I could make work for locks, some nylon twine, and a couple of knives. Dom brought his gun, just in case, and I had my multi-tool because I'd put it in my jacket pocket. We had our bulletproof vests in

the trunk, and I insisted that Taylor Thompson wear one.
The gesture helped Eldin relax, but it made Taylor a little
tense. I don't think he'd considered the danger real until
the moment he put it on.

We took off, with me still riding Dom's back. The plan
was for me to shift into raccoon form if something
happened or we were caught. We were far enough away
from the compound that I felt like we were probably safe.

We walked the property for about half a mile until we
came to the pond. We followed its edge poking sticks into
thicker parts of the brush trying to uncover a manhole or
some kind of cellar door. We'd had no luck by the time we
reached the wide mouth of the stream where it flowed into
the pond.

"Well, poop." I sighed. "I was hoping it would be easier
than this. A super-secret opening to an evil-lair is always
easy to find in the movies."

"Hey!" Eldin shouted. "What the hell was that?"

"What?" Dom asked.

"Quiet," Taylor hissed.

I heard it then. *Doo-ip, doo-ip, doo-ip*, and a small splash.
"There!" I pointed to where the water was rippling out
from four spots on the small lake. "Someone skipping
rocks."

Skipping rocks on the lake. Damn that Sunny Trimmel.
She was three for three.

"Help," a weak voice called out. "Help me."

"The stream," Eldin shouted. "It's coming from the
stream."

Dom practically dropped me on the ground, his gun

raised and ready. "Taylor, you stay with Nic. Eldin and I will go check it out."

I hopped in his direction. I wasn't missing whatever was happening. I didn't get far before Dom came rushing back to me. His eyes were haunted as if he'd seen a ghost. "It's Lieberman. He's barely hanging on."

"We need to get him to Doctor Smith right now," I said, my adrenaline raising my voice an octave.

"Eldin is calling your dad and the sheriff's department to get emergency vehicles out here, but Lieberman's foot is caught in a bear trap under the water. He's half frozen, and the water is neck high. I put a stick down, and it hit another trap. I don't know how many are out there.

"Coil spring, long spring, or conibear?"

"The one I triggered was a long spring, but I don't know what kind trapped Lieberman."

"Get me there," I told him. "I can swim out to him without activating the traps, dive down and unlock the claws on his feet."

"But how? Especially if you don't know which kind of trap he's caught in."

"I have twine, a multi-tool, and a raccoon's opposable thumbs." I wiggled my fingers at him. "My dad had taught me how to get out of any bear trap if I was ever caught in one. I'll cut a length and tie it to my multi-tool. That's all I'll need."

"If you have any problems at all, you get the hell out of the water. I want to save Lieberman, but not at your expense."

I kissed his worried face. "I'll stay safe."

At the edge of the creek, I watched Lieberman struggle to keep his head above water. "Hang in there. I'm coming to help. Just hold on a while longer."

"I don't know if I can," he said. "I'm so tired. I just want to sleep."

I stripped my shirt off, and Dom braced me up as I slid my palazzo pants off one leg at a time.

"This wasn't what I imagined when I thought about getting you naked."

I covered his lips with my finger. "Don't make this any more awkward for me."

I shifted, and Dom handed me my tool on the string. I grabbed the string and dragged the tool down into the water with me. I kept to the surface until I got to Lieberman.

"I'm not cold anymore," he said, his words slurring. Crap, he was suffering from hypothermia, and God knew what else.

I dove down, the water dark and murky, and felt for the trap. Damn it. It was a conibear, one of the most dangerous traps out there. Whoever laid these in the creek was not messing around. I surfaced for a breath of air then went back down feeling for the upper and lower loops. I threaded the twine through the top loop then down through the bottom loop and back up into the top loop just like Dad had taught me.

Then I swam up as hard as I could to pull it open, but I was yanked back for my efforts and dropped my tool and the twine. I surfaced for air then went back down again. I positioned my stepped on the chain of the trap, found the twine, and tried again.

I couldn't budge it. I wasn't strong enough as a raccoon to hold the trap down and pull up on the string at the same time. All I was doing was killing Lieberman faster.

I surfaced again, shifted, and let out a frustrated scream. Dom shouted my name.

"Don't come in! There are traps everywhere!" I warned.

Lieberman's head slid under water.

No, no, no. Oh, God, he wasn't going to make it, all because I wasn't strong enough. No, I thought, I won't give up. Not on Lieberman and not on myself. I lifted his chin, getting his face out of the water. "Come on, buddy. You have a pregnant wife at home that needs her husband." I gave him a breath before inhaling deeply and diving under again. It was harder to concentrate without the extra layer of fur, but I managed to find the twine again. I pressed down on the chain on either side with my feet and pulled up on the string with all my might. It was slowly opening. I only hoped I could get Lieberman free before I ran out of breath, and he ran out of time.

Finally, the damn thing opened enough for me to yank Lieberman's foot out of the trap. I let it go, and it snapped shut. I swam up. Lieberman was passed out, and he'd stopped breathing. "I've got him," I shouted. I swam on my back, keeping the poor man above me and away from the other traps. I kept going like that until we were at the shore and Dom hauled us both out.

Breathlessly, I said, "He needs to be resuscitated." Lights and sirens roared in the distance as Eldin and Taylor performed CPR on him. I prayed to anyone listening to save him. To not let him die. When Lieberman started coughing and throwing up water, all good signs, I started laughing, and then crying, as Dom rocked me in his arms.

As the police vehicles roared into the field near the pond, I looked up at my green-eyed rock, and said, "How in the world are we going to explain this to Dad?"

Dom kissed me. "I think he'll forgive you this time."

I shook my head. "You obviously don't know my father."

CHAPTER NINETEEN

*L*ieberman was taken to Doctor Smith. He'd had several strips of skin missing from his torso and back, his right pinky toe had been cut off, and the bear trap had dug into his leg pretty deep, so he'd lost a lot of blood. Having it happen in cold water had actually saved his life by slowing down the flow. Although, if he hadn't stepped into a trap at all, he'd have probably been back home. The call to his wife had shaken me. She'd cried hard racking sobs of relief, and I'll admit, I teared up. That he was alive was hopeful, but he hadn't woken up since his heart stopped. Doctor Smith worried he might have suffered some brain damage due to hypoxia.

We gave our statements to my dad, who told Eldin if he was "so fired up to work on his time off, then he could take first watch at the clinic to keep Lieberman safe."

Poor Eldin. Taylor didn't get off any easier, his brother Tyler laid into him hard for getting himself "involved in a dangerous game, and the fact that you are wearing a bulletproof vest should have told you just how stupid your actions were." Taylor didn't look one bit phased by his twin. Instead, after the heavier brother finished his rant, Taylor put his hand on Tyler's shoulder said, "It's okay, bro. I'm okay." They hugged it out. It was all very sweet...Until dad turned his attention on me. Oy.

After several hours of getting my butt handed to me by my dad first, then later at home by my mom, I took a hot shower, put on my warmest flannel pajamas, and crawled into my childhood bed. I'd freaking saved a man tonight. I was not going to feel bad about it.

However, I did feel bad for Dom. His plan to get on my parents' good side was failing miserably. Still, Lieberman was safe, and that as all that mattered right this minute.

Mom opened my bedroom door and sat next to me on the bed. She combed her fingers through my hair. "You know you scared your dad, right?"

"I'm sorry, Mom. I'm sorry that I worry him, but he's going to have to let that go. I'm not a child anymore. I'm a trained agent, a law enforcement officer just like he is, and people depend on me. My job puts me in the line of fire, and that's something that Dad is going to have to learn to deal with."

"You will always be our child, and no matter how rational you want to be about your choice to integrate and work for the FBI, it doesn't change how we see you or how we love you. One of these days you'll have your own kids, and you will know exactly what we mean."

"You mean, I'll be punished for putting you all through the ringer."

"No, I mean you'll be blessed to know a love that you would give up your life for. Your dad almost sacrificed his job for you the last time you were in town. He and I would do anything to protect you. That's both the joy and the bane of parenthood."

I nodded. "Is Dad still awake?"

Mom offered me a sad smile. "Wait until morning to talk to him. The world always looks a little brighter with the sunrise."

"Thanks, Mom."

She kissed my forehead. "I love you, Puddin'."

THE RATTLING WINDOW pane woke me up at two in the morning. Another rainstorm had kicked up during the night. I lay there awake, the covers tucked up under my chin, for what felt like hours but according to my digital clock had only been seven minutes.

I couldn't stop thinking about dessert pastries and Dom. Both delicious ideas and I needed to satisfy at least one of my cravings. I opted for the sweet rolls since they were less complicated. Decision made, I eased out of bed and moved as quietly as my damaged ankle would allow from my bedroom to the hall and downstairs to the kitchen trying not to wake up the whole house. The pain pills had kicked in, and between them and my own bodies ability to heal quickly, I wasn't hurting much.

The sweet rolls were under a floured cloth in a pan. I

grabbed a glass from the cabinet above the sink and got some milk from the fridge.

"The doctor said you weren't supposed to put any weight on that foot."

I fumbled the glass of milk in my hand, spilling half of it on the floor. "Damn it, Dom. You scared the crap out of me."

"I wasn't being sneaky, unlike a certain raccoon I know." He grabbed a paper towel off the roll and cleaned up the mess I'd made. "Your dad lit into you pretty hard. You okay?"

"He's just worried about me."

Dom took my roll and glass of milk from me and set it on the small table in the kitchen. "I can relate." He gave me a lopsided grin. "Why do they call you, Puddin'?"

"Oh, that." I shook my head. "Apparently, when I was around two-years-old my folks found me out in the yard after a hard rain eating mud and happily squealing, *pudding*! It became my nickname." I sat down across from him. "I'm just glad I wasn't shouting, poop!"

Dom laughed. It was warm and rich. I noticed he wore a light blue T-shirt, one of those super soft almost translucent ones, and a pair of drawstring pajama bottoms. I fantasized as I chewed the sweet bread about untying the rabbit ears' bow and watching his pants fall to the floor. Bow-chicka-bow-wow.

The space between Dominic's brow creased. "What are you thinking about?"

"Uh, nothing, why?"

"You are humming." He raised a brow. "Nicole Rae

Taylor. If I didn't know any better, I'd say you were undressing me with your eyes."

I raised a brow back. "Then I guess you don't know me at all because that's exactly what I'm doing." I shoved another bite in my mouth and stood up. "I'd better get to bed."

Dom shook his head. "You're a hard woman, Nicole."

I limped around to his side of the table and sat on his knee. "And I can use a hard man." I traced his bottom lip with my index finger. "Now, are you going to take me to bed or what?"

"Your parents?" Dom said.

"Are not invited," I replied.

"They will hear us." There was a heated strain in his voice.

I shook my head. "No risk, no reward."

"But..."

I put my finger over both his lips. "If you don't want me, fine. I'll see you in the morning." I got up and started toward the stairs. I held my breath, not wanting to Dominic to see my disappointment. I knew he was right. Probably better not to risk pissing my dad off even more, but after the day we'd had...

I squeaked when Dom scooped me up into his arms. I wrapped my legs around his waist.

"Woman," he said, his voice so gravelly and growly it sent shivers up and down my skin. "I want you." He buried his face in my neck. "I want you so bad I can't think straight." The warmth of his lips on my collarbone sent shocks of pleasure through me. "I have wanted you every second of every day since you fell into my arms in that stupid parking lot." He kissed up my neck. I moaned at the feel of his mouth on me.

I weaved my fingers through his thick, short waves of hair. "Oh, God. Me too." He carried me down the hall to the guest bedroom and took me inside. He closed the door behind us with my back as he pushed me up against it with a thud. "Shhhh," I said, throwing my head back as his tongue dipped into the clef at the base of my neck.

He carried me to the bed and set me down, careful of my ankle. He glanced at me up and down then licked his lips. "That flannel nightgown is fulfilling all of my *Little House on the Prairie* fantasies."

"You want to be the Almonzo Wilder to my Laura Ingalls?"

"I want to the Dom to your Nic," he said softly.

My stomach did a somersault, two backflips, and a handstand. My mouth was so dry I could barely speak, but I managed to say, "Take off your clothes."

To say that watching Dom strip was transcendental would be giving transcendental way too much credit. It was beyond sublime. He slid his T-shirt over his head, and his wide chest was covered in a layer of soft, black hair that tapered at his diaphragm before trailing down his stomach and under the waist of his pajama bottoms. I sat up and reached out for the drawstring bow and gave it a slow tug.

Dom's eyes darkened as he knelt in front of me. His hands slid under my flannel nightgown, shoving the thick material up my thighs. "This isn't meaningless to me." He dipped his head and kissed my exposed knee as he spread my legs and moved his body between them. He pressed his lips to mine as he moved against me, his thick length pressed against my core through two layers of material, his bottoms, and my panties.

I rubbed my groin against him as his hands roamed my back. He reached under me and freed the nightgown, sliding it over my head and off my arms. He splayed his hand on my chest, his pale green eyes watching me carefully. "You are so goddamn beautiful it makes me ache."

My whole body clenched with pleasure. "I've never been with a therianthrope," I blurted out.

Dom frowned. "Not even Farraday?"

"God, no. You heard him. Gay. I guess he knew enough to stop seeing me when we got to the point where sex was next."

Dom's thumbs brushed my nipples making them go instantly rigid. He pressed his hard length against me as he wrapped one arm around my back. "Once you go black bear you'll never go back there."

I laughed. "Don't ever say that again."

He nodded. "Promise." He put his free hand on my chest and eased me back into an arch, his mouth clamping over my nipple. I lifted my legs, bending at the knees to give him more accesses. He reached down between us, his clever fingers slipping under the fabric of my underwear to tease my aching sex.

Jesus, this slow play was killing me. "I can't..." I panted. "I can't..."

Dom stopped what he was doing and stared at me as if

I'd punched him in the gut. "If you're not ready, we can wait. I'll wait as long as you want. Just don't say we can't."

I took a deep breath and tried to settle myself to finish the thought. "I. Can't. Wait." I reached over and hooked my thumbs on his waistband and tugged his pajama bottoms down until he sprung out at me like a loaded cannon. "I need you, Dom. I need you right now."

I tried to squirm out of my underwear, but his body and legs, and arm, and everything was impeding my ability to get naked.

I let out a frustrated noise that turned to triumph when Dom reached down and ripped them clean off me. It hurt for a second, but not in any way that spoiled the moment. He lifted my legs and drove himself into me. I grunted and moaned as his girth split me wide open. I could feel every inch of him as he moved. God, he was so big, more than I'd bargained for, and it took a moment for the pain to convert to pleasure. I wrapped a leg behind his back, my hands finding purchase as I clawed at his shoulders.

"Am I hurting you?" he asked.

"Yes," I whispered, tears leaking from my eyes. "Please, don't stop. Don't stop."

He wrapped me tighter in his arms as his lower half continued its erotic assault. My body went hot and tingly as I felt the first bright burn of an orgasm building inside me.

"Nicole," he murmured. "Yes, yes." He groaned. "You feel so good. So good."

The bright burning turned my body into a pressure

181

cooker in need of a serious quick release. "Ah!" I cried out. My back bowed as I shuddered against Dom's chest, unable to do anything other than ride the wave of ecstasy. His fingers tightened on my shoulders as his thrusting became shorter, quicker, more insistent, and then he groaned on one final hard thrust, as he climaxed right after me.

He held himself above me for a moment, wiping the tears from the sides of my face. "I promised it wouldn't be quick." A sweet smile played on his lips. "I lied."

"Next time," I said. "God, I love looking at your face."

"I love looking at your face," he said back. His gaze narrowed at me, suddenly serious. "Make no mistake, Nicole. I'm falling in love with you."

"I..."

Knock! Knock! Knock!

The loud, angry knock on the door had Dom rolling off the bed and me grabbing for my gown. My dad's voice penetrated the room. "Farraday called. Your victim is awake and talking."

CHAPTER TWENTY

*R*ay Lieberman sat up in bed, his skin pale and his face gaunt with extreme dehydration and malnourishment. His wife, a small, pear-shaped woman with a basketball-sized baby pooch for a belly.

"My sister is watching our children," she said, grasping Lieberman's hand as if it were the only thing tethering her to the ground. "Thank you so much, Agent Taylor. You and Agent Tartan have given me back my life." She began to cry. "My life."

"Bunny," Lieberman said softly. "Don't cry. I'm okay. I'm safe now."

She sniffed hard then nodded.

"Mister Lieberman, I need to ask you a few questions. I'm sorry it has to be so soon after you've been reunited with your wife, but every minute we wait gives your abductor the opportunity to cover his tracks," Dominic said. "This guy has been ten steps ahead of us the whole time."

"But not tonight," Lieberman said. He gave us a faint smile. "Ask your questions."

Dom looked at the man's wife. "Mrs. Lieberman, would you wait in the hall until we're done?"

"No," she said with such emphatic determination. "I'm not letting this man out of my sight. Not for a solitary second."

"It's okay, ma'am." I gave Dom a nod. "You can stay."

"Can you describe the man who took you?"

Lieberman closed his eyes for a moment. When he opened them back up, he gave a slight shake of his head. "He wore a hood. I never saw his face."

Dom passed me a look of disappointment. "Anything identifiable? Height, weight, hair color, eye color, scars, tattoos, anything."

"His eyes," Lieberman said. "They were strange."

"Strange how? Overly large. The color? Shape?"

"The color. They were really light, almost colorless, but not the pink-white of an albino. I have a cousin whose albino, and this was different."

Weird, almost colorless eyes? Dom and I both said, "Lark."

I nodded. "It makes sense. He has access to the compound, and he has the hallmarks of a psychopath."

"He struck me from above. I managed to see his shadow on my steps, so I'd ducked and turned." He touched the bruised and cracked bridge of his nose. "Whatever he had hit my nose. I tried to fight, but he managed to get his hand around my mouth and nose. The rag he put over my face smelled like chemicals, but it wasn't unpleasant. It had kind of sweet scent."

"Ether, maybe," I said.

Doctor Smith joined us in the room. He gave his patient a sympathetic look. "How are you feeling, Ray?"

"Better. The salve you put on the cuts has made them feel a lot less painful."

Everyone in these parts knew the secret to the doc's ointment. It was lycanthrope spit. Apparently, the saliva of a lycanthrope had industrial strength antibodies that not only numbed pain but also sped healing exponentially. There wasn't a home in Peculiar that didn't have a small tin of his wonder-drug.

The doc looked at Dom and me. "Can I talk to you both in the other room for a moment? I think Ray and his wife could both use the break."

We followed the tall werewolf back to his office. He closed the door behind us. "I can tell you both, now that I've been able to examine one of the Little Piggy victims, that the person who tortured Ray Lieberman is the same person who killed Lloyd Evans. The cuts were made with the same kind of blade."

"Are you sure?" Dom asked.

"Yes. There is a small defect in the blade that causes a small, jagged tear at the starting point. It's the same on Lloyd's defensive wounds and the slashes across his torso."

"Then our guy is scared. Evans must have stumbled onto him somehow," Dom said.

"Or," I added, playing Devil's advocate, "Evans was the

unsub's partner in crime, and he killed him to tie up loose ends."

"Maybe." Dom crossed his arms. "We need to ask Lieberman what he can remember and see if there was more than one person involved. It could be crucial. If Evans was in close contact with the killer, it points even more to Andy Lark."

"Is there anything else, Doc?"

The silver-haired wolf nodded. "The toothpick you found. It matches Lloyd's teeth marks. I think when and if the DNA arrives back from the Springfield lab, it will confirm that Evan's was down in that room."

Dad had served the warrant on the compound after we'd found Lieberman. They didn't find any weapons, but they did find the room exactly where we'd told him it would be. "I wonder if the forensics will find DNA of the other victims down there."

"Only time will tell." The doctor looked tired. "You two go talk to Lieberman. I've got a few more things to do before I call it a night."

When we walked back into the patient's room, Lieberman's wife had crawled into bed next to him. "I'm sorry," I said. "I know you both are tired, and you're ready for this whole nightmare to be over, but we have a few more questions."

"I'll tell you what I can remember. Unfortunately," he squeezed his eyes shut for a moment, "or maybe, fortunately, I can't remember a lot of the first couple of days. The man kept saying something about me having a bad reaction to the drug he gave me."

"Was he saying it to you or someone else?" Dom asked.

"I...I'm not sure. There could have been someone else."

"It's important." Dominic took a step toward him. "The man who took you, we think he might have been working with someone else. If it's true, we might be able to make more connections."

I put my hand on Dom's arm. I didn't want him planting memories that didn't exist in Lieberman's head. Victims were often susceptible to confabulation, or false memories, especially if there were gaps in their recollections. Their brains would grasp at the solutions offered and use that to fill in the blanks. We needed the real story, not one that we invented.

"If you don't remember anyone else, that's fine," I said gently. "We're going to find this bastard either way, and we will make sure he never hurts another soul."

"I wish I could remember more. I promise if I recall anything else I will tell someone immediately." Ray put his arm around his wife's shoulders. "I'm really tired."

"We'll let you rest," Dom said. "Thank you for your time and patience."

Ray looked up at us, his dark blue eyes shining with a tear. "Thank you, both of you, for saving my life."

WE DROVE STRAIGHT TO the Sheriff's Station, managing to beat Dad back from the compound. We parked and waited outside for him to arrive with Andy Lark in cuffs. I couldn't wait to get justice for his victims.

How long had he been killing? How many more victims besides the four we knew about? Andy was probably in his sixties—young for shifters, but a long time all the same, especially for a murdering bastard like Lark. There was no way the recent victims were his first kills. Either he practiced his sick art elsewhere, or he'd changed his MO. Why? I hoped we would find out before therian justice was handed down. Unfortunately, some psychopaths never revealed their secrets. It was another way to continue taking pleasure in their victims' pain long after they left this life.

I saw my dad's truck and patted the hood to get Dom's attention. "There they are."

Dom let out a noisy exhalation.

"Oh, stop worrying. It's not like Dad's going to arrest you for defiling his daughter."

Dom quirked his head at me. "Then maybe I didn't do it right."

I smacked him. "You can try again later."

He chuckled but sobered quickly when Dad got out of the driver's seat, opened the back door and escorted Lark, hands cuffed behind his back, out of the vehicle.

Lark's expression was smug, his colorless eyes as cold as a glacier. It was clear to me that he considered this whole thing one big joke. It galled me to no end that a psychopath who couldn't feel empathy or guilt had no problems feeling joy. He could take pleasure in the pain of others. To him, victims were no more than toys—and when he was done, they become broken objects to be discarded like so much trash.

"Every time I see that guy I want to beat the shit out of him," Dom said.

I thought the same thing. "He is the epitome of douche-nozzle."

"You have a magical way with words." He nodded toward my dad, who was walking behind Lark toward the station. "We better catch up."

My ankle hurt even less than the night before, so I barely limped. Dad glanced back at me. His eyes softened for a moment. I smiled. Maybe my father wasn't too upset about Dom and me.

Andy Lark began to shake and flail. Dad tried to hold on to the prisoner, but Lark sprouted huge wings full of brown, white, and black feathers. The cuffs shattered, dropping to the ground as the creature rounded on my father.

Dad didn't let his surprise overcome his training. He immediately tried to unlatch his gun.

Too late.

"What the hell is that?" Dom shouted. We were both running toward Dad and his assailant, guns drawn.

Lark had completely shifted into the biggest owl I've ever seen. He rose into the air, huge talons aimed at Dad.

My father didn't have a chance.

Horror welled in me as the nightmare unfolded in slow motion. The bird's sharp claws embedded into Dad's chest —and the massive bird beat its wings, using the momentum to tear open flesh. With one final slash at Dad's neck, Lark screeched in triumph. Dad fell to the ground, his shirt in shreds, his face and chest bloody.

So much blood.

"I don't have a shot," Deputy Thompson shouted. He was behind the truck, pistol pointed toward the birdman.

I heard my own shouts as if I were listening to them through water. Lark launched himself into the air. As if outside my body, I saw my arm fully extend as I discharged my weapon at the winged creature. Mine wasn't the only shots I heard. Dom and Thompson shot at the escaping prisoner as well, and we didn't stop until our guns were empty.

Feathers floated around us like ugly snowflakes. Lark screeched and tumbled to the ground. He gave one last gasp before he stilled. He was dead, but I damned sure wished I could kill him again. The acrid smell of gunpowder filled the air. My ears throbbed from loud reports of the gun. And my heart wanted to punch out of my chest.

The mind fog lifted, and I focused on my dad's limp body. "Dad!" I screamed. I didn't feel the pain in my ankle as I ran and dropped to the ground beside him. Thompson was kneeling next to Dad holding pressure over the wound on my dad's neck. Deep, long gashes marred my Dad's chest, and blood flowed like rivers down his side, pooling on the ground.

Panic made my whole body shake as I grabbed my father's hand. Dad's eyes were closed. There was some mercy in my father being unconscious. "Did it hit his artery?" I asked Thompson.

"I don't know." His face was haunted, and for the first time, to me, he looked impossibly young.

Dom put his hand on my shoulder, and I heard him talking on the phone. "We need you here now," he said. "The sheriff is badly injured. We can't move him—he's not stable enough. Hurry, Doc." He squeezed my shoulder. "Doctor Smith is on the way, Nic."

"Please, Dad," I begged. "Stay with me." His respirations were shallow and rapid. Little gurgling sounds escaped as bubbles formed on dad's chest. "Dom," I said, saying his name like a last prayer. I didn't know what I expected him to do, but I knew his presence was the only thing keeping me from losing my shit completely.

"I've seen this before. He has an open pneumothorax," Dom said. He ran to the car and grabbed one of the rain ponchos. When he returned, he used a small pocketknife and cut a square in the plastic. "Here, put the hole over the area with the bubbles. It will occlude the wound and stop blood from getting sucked into the chest. We have to hold it on down on three sides."

I nodded, snot and tears running down my face. Dom knelt next to me and used his shirt to wipe my nose. Then he pressed on two sides of the poncho. I pushed on the remaining one. Thompson had both of his hands clamped over my dad's neck.

"The doctor's coming, Nic," reassured Dom. "Your dad is strong. He'll make it."

Dad didn't look strong. Not right now. He looked like a dying man. Not my dad, I thought. Not him. He's Superman. Indestructible.

It took seven minutes for Doctor Smith arrived with

his fiancé Chavvah. It had been the longest seven minutes of my entire existence.

Doc and Chavvah worked together to stabilize my dad for transport.

"You can let go," said Chavvah gently. "We're going to put an occlusive bandage on his chest. It's designed for this type of wound."

I hadn't even noticed that Dom had already moved his hand from the poncho. For some reason, I couldn't get my hands to move. My sensitive fingertips could barely register the plastic because they were so coated with blood.

Dom placed his hands over mine, and I let him help me release the poncho.

While Chavvah worked on my dad's chest, Doc Smith had taken Thompson's place and was wrapping some kind of bandage under my Dad's armpit and then over his neck. "It's an Israeli pressure bandage," he explained, his voice kind. "Thompson, bring me the neck brace."

After Doc stabilized my dad's neck, we all helped move Dad onto the spine board.

They loaded him into the back of Dad's truck, and I got in, too. Before they shut the doors, I said, "Call my mom, Dom. She has to know. He can't..." I shook my head. "She needs to know."

"Consider it done." He looked torn, and I understood why. He needed to call in Lark's death and handle the scene. But I could see he was ready to chuck it all just to be with me. The idea that he cared about me more than he did the job was something of a balm.

"Stay," I said. "I'll call you with updates."

"I get there as soon as I can." He shut the doors, and Doc Smith pointed the truck toward the clinic to be the longest drive of my life.

WHEN WE ARRIVED AT the clinic, my mother stood in Doc's parking lot, her face as pale as a ghost's. The deputy helped Doc Smith get my dad onto a gurney and get him inside. Mom held Dad's hand but stayed out of the way. I felt numb. Nothing about this was real. Nothing.

When the doc took him back for emergency surgery, my mom's shoulders slumped. She turned to me. "Your dad is a fighter," she said. "He'll be okay."

"I know." I took her hand. "Let's go sit down somewhere."

Chavvah greeted us in the small waiting room. "Why don't y'all come into the house? I'll make you all some coffee or tea, whatever you'd like, while we wait."

My mom looked down the hall to the door where Doc had taken my father. "I don't want to leave him."

Chav put her hand on my mom's back. "And you won't be, Jean. Let me take care of you while Billy Bob takes care of Sid."

My mom's stoic expression cracked. She nodded. "Okay."

I took a staggered breath trying to stop more tears and cast Chavvah a grateful look.

Mom and I huddled together on the couch for two hours, dying with every minute that passed. The time gave me a chance to reflect on the Sunny's predictions. So far, there had been the gunshot with the yellow man, the crack that tripped a trap door, the skipping stones that alerted us to Lieberman, and now Andy Lark had transformed into a gigantic lying owl. But her predictions hadn't stopped there. She'd also predicted something about glass breaking and death at twelve. I looked at the clock. It was ten-thirty in the morning. If the doctor kept my dad in surgery past noon, I was storming damn the clinic.

It was half an hour later when the doctor finally came into the house, his face grave.

I scooted to the edge, waiting with fear and trepidation.

"It was touch and go," Doc said, "but Sid is one tough son-of-a-gun. He's going to make a full recovery."

"Jesus, Doc," I said with no small amount of exasperation. "Don't bury the lead."

A noise that sounded like a wounded animal startled me to my feet. I looked at my mom as her shoulders heaved forward, and she began to sob. "Thank you, Doctor Smith. Thank you."

I put my arms around Mom. I suddenly realized when the crisis was in full swing, she'd done what she always does —put on a brave face to protect me. Here she had been, her husband, her great love possibly dying, and instead of falling apart, she had kept it together for me. The realization made me proud of her and ashamed of myself.

I turned to the doctor. "Can we see him?"

Doc nodded. "Yes. He's not awake yet, but it will be good for him to see family when he does."

"Thanks, Doc." To Mom, I said, "You are the bravest woman I know," I told her with a fierceness I felt to my core. "You are my hero." I gave her another squeeze. "Now, let's go see my other hero."

CHAPTER TWENTY-ONE

*I*t was late afternoon by the time my dad woke up. Dom had texted to let me know that an advisor from the Tri-State Council was on her way down to help us spin the story for the FBI about the death of Andrei Lark, the Little Piggy killer. There were so many things we would never understand about the man, but as I looked at my father, I couldn't bring myself to care. That man had destroyed so many families, and he'd almost destroyed mine. He could rot in Hell with all the other dead psychos.

"Hey, Puddin'," Dad said, his voice weak.

I took his hand. "Hi, Dad."

"Did that worm-eating bastard get away?"

"Turns out that a bird can't fly when he's filled with lead."

My dad chuckled then started coughing. "Ow, ow."

"Don't laugh," Jean said. "You'll undo all the doctor's

good work." She took Dad's other hand. Her voice lowered. "You scared twenty years off my life, Sid."

"I'm sorry, sweetheart. I didn't mean to frighten you." He brought her fingers to his lips. "I'm okay, though." He winced. "At least, I will be. Billy Bob says so, so it must be true." He patted my mother's cheek. "You look tired, Jeanie girl. Why don't you go home and rest?"

"I'll rest when I'm dead, Sidney." Mom's tone was sharp and cutting. "If you're not home then I'm not home. I've already told Doctor Smith to bring me a cot."

Dad looked befuddled. "I can scoot over if you want to share a bed." He pulled her down for a kiss.

"Gross," I said.

Dad narrowed his gaze at me. "You're one to talk."

"Touché." I leaned over and kissed his cheek. "Are we good?"

Dad gave me a short nod. "You're a grown woman, Nicole, and a capable agent. I'm sorry if I've been treating you like a child. I'm trying. I promise."

"I know, Dad. And, really, I've been just as bad. I am a competent, intelligent, mature woman until I get around you and mom, and then I turn into a rebellious sixteen-year-old trying to show you two just how independent I am."

"We don't help." Mom smiled at me. "You're a beautiful woman, Nicole. Smart and accomplished. We're proud of you."

"Even though I joined the FBI?"

Dad shook his head. "Yes, even though. We can't live

your life for you, Puddin'. All we can do is love you while you do it."

"Thanks." I stood up. "It looks like you two have it under control here. I'm going to go see if I can help Dom get this Little Piggy story sorted before we turn in our official report."

"Give Agent Tartan a message for me."

"Dad..." I didn't know if Mom knew or not about our dalliance in the guest room, but as far as I was concerned, I'd never be grown up enough for this conversation.

He took my hand before I could leave. "Tell him he better be the partner you deserve."

I grinned. "I'll tell him."

MOM GAVE ME THE KEYS to her car, one of those new models with the keyless entry and starter button. I took me a couple of seconds to figure the damn thing out, but once I did, I found that I really like the backup camera. My phone, in voice activation mode, connected to the car via Bluetooth, and I said, "Call Dominic."

My phone announced loudly over the car speakers, "There is no Dominic in your contacts."

"Oh, shoot." I grimaced. "Call Agent Pain in My Ass."

"Calling Agent Pain in My Ass."

I made a mental note to edit my contact. The phone rang once, and Dominic picked up. "How's your dad?"

"He's going to be okay." Saying the words out loud and

to Dom opened a floodgate inside me. "I don't know what I would have done if..."

"I know, darling. I'm so glad he's recovering. Are you staying with him and your mom?"

"No. I'm on my way to you. Where are you meeting with the Tri-State Council advisor?"

"She's here now." He sounded anxious. "Bethany Hilliard. She's a real piece of work. I can definitely use your help."

My phone beeped. A call came in from a local number. "Hold on, Dom." I didn't know how to use the voice thingy for switching calls, so I reached out and hit the "put current call on hold and answer call" option.

"Agent Taylor," I answered.

"Yes, Agent Taylor. This is Judge Holt. I hate to bother you, what with Sid being injured and all."

"How did you get my number?"

"You mom gave it to Judy. I hope you don't mind me calling, but Mallory Evans is in my chambers, and she refuses to leave until you come speak with her."

"Why?"

"She says she has some information about Andy Lark and the death of her cousin Lloyd. She refuses to speak to anyone but you. I think the overnight in jail really spooked her. I've given her a drink to calm down, but she seems shook."

"Okay," I said. "I'll let Dom know, and then I'll head on over."

"Good, good. How's Sid doing? Your mom told Judy that the surgery went well."

"He's doing better." I gave a happy sigh of relief. "I'll tell him you asked about him."

"I'll try to get out there today or tomorrow and see him."

"I'm sure he'd appreciate it. I'll see you in a few minutes."

I clicked the phone back over and took Dominic off hold. "You still there?"

"Yep. Who was it?"

"I'm going to see Judge Holt about a whack-a-doodle. Mallory Evans is with him, and she says she has some information about Andy Lark. Something to do with Lloyd Evans' death."

"Maybe I should meet you over there."

"It won't take two of us, and it sounds like you have your hands full with Miss Hilliard."

"That's not a lie. Okay, but if it might impact our official report, make sure you call me."

"I will."

"Nicole."

"Yes."

"Call me even if it doesn't have an impact."

I smiled. "You got it."

The drive to the courthouse was surprisingly smooth. Mom's car had a great suspension. The sound system blasted mom's classic rock-n-roll, and I'd jammed the last three minutes to AC/DC's *For Those About to Rock* song as I parked on the street in front of the old building. Damn, I wanted to keep this car.

I put my phone in my jacket pocket before I exited,

humming as I walked up the concrete steps and through the original wood front doors. The tune echoed in the halls, so I stopped. No need to embarrass myself with bad singing. The building was old brick and mortar with tiled floors. I stopped at the clerk's desk and rang the bell. "Can I help you?" Winifred Davis asked as she walked in from a back office. "Oh, Nicole Taylor. So nice to see you, dear."

"Hi, Mrs. Davis. I'm here to see Judge Holt. He's expecting me."

"His office is down the hallway. Go through the court-room all the way to the back and enter the door on the left side. There are three offices—the judge's chambers is the last door on the right."

"Thanks."

I flashed my badge at court security. I didn't have my gun. I'd left it at the scene so Dom could take it, along with his and Thompson's, for processing. Yay, FBI protocols.

The courtroom was eerily spooky. I'd spent some time at the Kansas City courthouse watching a few trials, just to get a feel for the procedure. Honestly, courtrooms, in general, gave me the creeps—even when they were filled with people. After I went through the first door, I found myself in a narrow hallway. When I got to the third door on the right, I knocked. No one answered so I tried the knob. It turned easily, so I stepped inside the chambers without an invite.

"Judge Holt? You back here?"

No answer. The room was majestic—just like a judge's chambers should like. It was tidy enough to wonder if the judge or housekeeping suffered from OCD. A handcrafted cherry wood executive desk and chair were the center-pieces. Shelves of law books lined one wall. Another wall was filled with his degree and awards as well as pictures of him with important people. Huh. There was a photo of him and Emmanuel Cleaver, who used to be the mayor of Kansas City, but was now a congressman. There was even one with him and Scott Bakula, the guy from *Quantum Leap*. My mom had had the biggest crush on that guy.

"I met Scott at a fundraiser in St. Louis. He was kind enough to pose with me."

I jumped because the judge had come into the room like a ninja. "Dang, Judge Holt. You almost gave me a heart attack."

"I'm sorry, Nicole. Your mother would never forgive me." He smiled. He was dressed in an immaculately tailored charcoal gray suit with a pinstripe gray and light purple button-down shirt, a burgundy tie, cuff links, and a pair of black Italian dress shoes. Fancy. "Thanks for coming."

"Where's Mallory?" I asked.

"I had to show her where to find the ladies room. It can be a little tricky in this old building. It's easy to get lost."

"I can imagine." I looked at a few more of the photographs. "You sure have met a lot of people." I saw one of a woman with bright eyes. The photo was black and white. She stood next to a boy with those same bright eyes. "Who's this?"

I turned to see him standing closer to me. "My mom,"

the judge said. His dark eyes were distant. Sad. "She was a beauty, wasn't she?"

"She really was," I agreed. "Was this taken out of the TSS property?"

"Yes," he said. "Shortly after my father died. She was determined to make a life for us there."

I'd noticed at my parents' house that Holt had tensed when my dad mentioned the judge's father. He'd done it again just now. "How did your dad die, if you don't mind me asking?"

"I don't mind." His body language said he minded a lot, but he was trying to appear relaxed. "Truth is, I don't remember what happened to him. I was young. My mother told me he had a heart attack."

I looked at the clock. What was Mallory doing? How long did it take to go to the toilet? I glanced at the judge and noticed something I hadn't before. "That's a nice tie clip, sir."

He fingered the metal strip across his tie, it had a duplicate pattern to the metal we'd found down in that basement cellar. "It belonged to my father."

"Was it part of a set?"

"Yes." He furrowed his brow. "How did you know?"

My stomach knotted. "Do you think Mallory got lost on her way back? Maybe I should go find her."

The judge walked to his desk, his face blank as he studied me. "You really are a smart girl, Nicole. Your mother and father always say so. I guess they're right." He opened a wooden box, usually reserved for gavels, but what he retrieved was a gun. "So smart."

I swallowed hard. I tried to appear cool even though my heart started pounding. "Is Mallory Evans really here?"

He nodded. "She is, and you're about to join her."

It was a stretch to make the judge fit my original ideas about the Little Piggy killer. Andy Lark was a much better match. But the judge had traveled for awards and charity events. The pictures on his wall proved that he was out of town enough to carry out the abductions. He was charming, almost superficially so, and he'd grown up on that compound. But still, I'd known him my whole life. He and my dad were friends.

"Was I a part of your plan, Judge? You only kill men, right? If you're the Little Piggy killer, then why pick me?"

"Because you are the easiest to explain away." He gestured with the gun for me to move to the back of the room. He flipped a switch inside the bookcase, and one section opened like a door. Inside the dark room, Mallory Evans was gagged and tied up on the floor. Her eyes bulged with absolute fear. I noted the bruise on the right side of her face. She was beyond terrified. As much as I didn't like the woman, she didn't deserve to be beaten and trussed up.

"My partner knows I'm here. In fact, he's probably on the way right now."

The judge tsked. "I know everything that goes on in Peculiar, little missy. Special Agent Dominic Tartan has his hands full with the Tri-Council rep. That Ms. Hilliard is harder than a barrel full of tacks. Why do you think I requested her as the liaison?" He kept the gun trained on my chest. "Get inside."

I did as he asked and he shut the secret door behind us.

The dim glow of the bulb cast a sickly yellow over the small concrete room. Mallory remained still. Only her eyes moved—switching between the judge and me.

"I am sorry it's come to this," he said. "I know Jean and Sid will be devastated." His smile was feral. "But you know what they say—time heals all wounds."

Judge Holt wasn't sorry at all. I'd bet he'd never been contrite in his entire life. Lucky for me, the judge's psychopathy included a heavy dose of narcissism. If I could keep him talking, it might give me time to find a way out of this mess. Given that he had the upper hand and we were secluded from prying eyes, I was guessing he'd be more than happy to gloat.

But first I had to attack his ego, just a little. He'd want to prove his superior intellect before he killed me. "You won't be able to fool Dominic. He'll have your number the minute you lie to him."

The judge's gaze flickered. "I've seen the way he looks at you, Nicole. That boy will be too torn up about Mallory killing you. You see, she took me hostage in my own office and demanded that I call you. As Andy Lark's lover, she's furious with you—enough to kill you."

"Yeah, that's brilliant all right," I said, adding just a touch of sarcasm to my voice. "Did she steal your gun first?"

"Oh, this?" Judge Holt preened. "Unregistered. I was raised TSS, remember? They don't register their guns. And they teach their children how to disarm marauding humans." He rolled his eyes. "Which will be how I saved my own life. Your death will be tragic, Mallory's will be deserved, and I'll be the hero."

The sheer arrogance of this man galled me. The fact that he was friends with my parents—and would continue that façade after he killed me—filled me with rage. *Stay calm. Stay focused. Stay alive.*

"Why do all this?" I asked. "We pinned Lark as the killer—you could have gotten away clean."

"Don't I know it!" He pointed the gun at Mallory. "The stupid girl really did come to me. She was with Lark the night her cousin died buying illegal guns. Evans wanted to militarize the TSS. Make sure we could defend ourselves against the humans. She knew he couldn't be the murderer." He chuckled. "You can imagine the dilemma. How did I get rid of her and keep your dad from investigating? The answer became obvious. If Mallory shot you dead, your dad and your boyfriend would be devastated. No point to an investigation. See? All wrapped up in a sweet little bow."

"Yeah. Okay. So that means you're done killing integrators?"

"No." He got a distant look in his eye. "My father was an integrator. He left my mother to go live with the humans. *He married one.* Can you imagine the shame my mother felt? We lived with the TSS. They let us stay in the compound, but we were outcasts. Because of him." Judge Holt shook his head. "She told me that my father was beset by demons. Male shifters who leave their real families to mate with female humans were all possessed. She showed me how to remove those demons." He held up his finger and a large white claw slide out from the tip. "She taught me how to sharpen my tool so we could relieve them of their sins."

I felt my stomach pitch. Psychopaths were born, sure, but they were also made—especially those awful few who became serial killers. "What did she do to you?" I asked softly.

"I had to carry on the work," he said in a faraway voice. "You have to strip the flesh. You have to dig deep into the muscle. Drill into bone. You have to make them scream. When they die, they're free." He blinked and turned his gaze to me. His eyes were dark and empty. This man had no soul. And he fucking scared the crap out of me. "Even though the demons are gone, they're not worthy of being returned into the fold. So, I take them back to their humans."

"You must've been disappointed that you couldn't excise Lieberman's demons."

The judge shrugged. "He had an allergic reaction to the chloroform. He was out of it most of the time. You can't exercise a man's demons if he's not conscious for the process."

"You spared him because he wasn't awake enough for you to enjoy his pain."

Judge Holt didn't answer, and I realized he was done talking. He had a stillness about him that made terror rip away my calm. My fight or flight instinct kicked in, and it took every ounce of willpower to stay put and keep silent.

I took a step back. My coat swung a little, and my phone bounced on my hip. Yes! Hurrah for smartphones with voice control. "You know what?" I raised my voice, "I call," I lowered my voice, "you," I raised it again, "Agent Pain in My Ass." The phone heard me and rewarded my efforts with a loud, "Calling Agent Pain in My Ass."

The judge's strange stupor evaporated. "What is that?" the judge asked. He rushed toward me.

"What's up, Puddin'?" The minute I heard Dom's voice I shouted, "It's Judge Holt! He's the kill—" was all I got out before the judge shot me. The bullet ripped through my shoulder throwing me back against the wall. Pictures dropped off the wall, and glass shattered around me. Oh, Jesus. *Glass falls.* Mallory screamed through her gag and tried to wiggle away, but the judge wasn't focused on her.

He only had eyes for me. And you know what I thought about? Sunny's predictions. Death was next. *Death strikes at twelve.*

The judge squatted next to me. "You little bitch," he said. He stuck his finger in my bullet wound and twisted. The pain made me light-headed, and I couldn't help but scream.

"Nic! Nicole!" Dominic's panicked voice distracted the judge for all of a second. Holt took the phone from my pocket and threw at the wall. It shattered—cutting off the only source of help I had. "We're going to have so much fun," he whispered as he dragged his bloodied finger down my cheek. "So much fun."

CHAPTER TWENTY-TWO

I felt sick to my stomach as Judge Holt carried me through a system of passages hidden in the courthouse walls. Mallory hadn't had a chance. He'd put the gun to the back of her head and pulled the trigger. I would never forget that horrifying moment. Murder was so profoundly gruesome—both physically and spiritually.

My multi-tool was in my front pocket. Problem was, he'd tied my wrists behind my back.

As we went along, it seemed the judge knew every secret nook and cranny the building possessed. The ropes he'd used to tie my wrists and ankles scratched my skin, and he'd stuffed my gunshot wound with gauze to slow the bleeding. He'd been serious about not killing me quick. I was both grateful and crazy scared.

"What happened to your father?" I asked him again. The question seemed to be the only one that evoked any real emotion from the man.

"I told you. He left my mom for an integrator because

he was possessed. She showed me how to release him from his sins."

I had no doubt there would be scars on his back from his mother's "training."

"You killed your father."

"I saved him." He continued moving, his voice once again flat. "Integrators have to repent first. But the demons are strong, and I have to cut away the flesh. Only then do the integrators confess. As their life force drains, I cut off the pinky toe so that the demons will leave the body."

Judge Holt might believe he cut off the pinky toes to release demons, but the reality was that those toes were also his trophies. I had no doubts that he had them stored somewhere.

We stopped, suddenly, but it was too dark for me to see. Judge Holt set me down on the dusty floor. He turned his gaze on me, and I recoiled at the sight of his white, glowing eyes.

"What are you?" I hadn't meant to sound frightened, but his gleeful response told me he'd enjoyed my fear.

"I'm *Scalapus humanus*. My animal is a version of the Eastern mole, but my species has developed eyes that can see better in the dark than in the light. I wear contacts when I have to be above ground to keep them protected."

"I've never heard of your kind."

"We're rare. Other than my parents, I've never met another like me." He moved close enough to my face that I could smell the sweet smell of whiskey on his breath.

He moved away and was doing something that I

couldn't see. I twisted my body, fighting to get my arms to bend enough to reach into my front pocket for the tool.

"What are you doing?" the judge asked. "You know I can see in the dark." He turned his spooky eyes on me. "Perfectly. You are in my world. You can't escape me."

"Leiberman did."

"Well, I had to kill Lloyd. After dumping the body, I returned to find that Lieberman had escaped. The man never saw my face. I wasn't worried about him identifying me." The judge made a noise of triumph. "There." He pulled a panel from the wall, and the corridor lit up.

When he shielded his eyes, I screamed as I kicked him at the knees and felt my ankle snap again. Holt bellowed his rage as he fell through the opening. Quickly, I closed my eyes and willed my animal forward. It would make me more vulnerable for a moment, but was my only hope of escaping the madman.

I changed easily, but now I was trapped in my clothes, tangled in a mess of pants, shirt, undergarments. When I got myself free, I looked up to see the judge's glowing eyes as he tried to hammer me with a gavel. I rolled as it hit the concrete. Cripes, the hammer end was metal and took a small chunk out of the floor where my head had just been. I engaged my legs as fast as they would carry me, which would typically have been close to fifteen miles per hour, but unfortunately, with the hurt ankle, I moved a little slower. I was blind as I flew down the secret path, trying to remember which way to turn to get back to the judge's quarters.

"Nicole!" the judge roared. "Nicole!"

If he thought I was going to answer him, he really was nuts. In the distance, I heard my name coming from the opposite direction. My pulse jumped as I realized it was Dom.

I'm here, I chittered in raccoon language, but not in any way he could hear me. I couldn't risk changing forms. Not with the judge hot on my trail. *Call my name again*, I willed Dom. *Call my name to guide me out of here.*

I hit a wall. No! I turned around to go back, but it was too late. I was trapped.

"I can see you, little Nicole," the judge said. I could see his glowing eyes about thirty feet away. "You can't escape me."

I took a deep breath, braced myself against the wall, and when the judge was less than four feet away, I pushed off in a fantastic leap, landing on the judge's face. I fought and scratched and bit him until all I could taste and see was his awful blood. He grappled at me with his hands, hitting me, yanking my tail, slicing at me with his claw, and doing everything in his power to get me off his head.

A roar that shook the walls of my prison froze the judge and me in place for the space of a heartbeat, before I dug my tiny fingers into his eyes. He screamed just as the wall beside us exploded and a giant black bear smashed through behind us.

I heard the clock tower in the courthouse building begin to chime. *Bong.* I jumped from the judge's head. Dom's bear clamped his jaws around the judge's neck and shook the man for eleven more *bongs*.

The judge stopped moving. And breathing.

Death strikes at twelve.

I shifted back to human. I huddled against the wall, revulsion, and disgust pummeling my gut as I wretched the blood from my throat. Dom ran his hands over me. "Are you okay, darling? Are you hurt? Did he hurt you? Talk to me? You're scaring me, Nic. Talk to me."

"I..." I hiccupped. "I'm okay." I started to cry when he put his arms around me. "I'm okay."

"Dominic, did you find her?" I heard Eldin yell.

I touched Dom's cheek as he held me so tight it was hard to breathe. "You called the cavalry, huh?"

"You betcha," Dom said. He squeezed me even more.

I let out a small cry of pain. "Careful." I touched my wounded shoulder.

"You're bleeding."

"That's because I've been shot. It hurts like hell, but I'm pretty sure I'm going to live."

"In here, I found her!" he hollered to Eldin with some urgency. "Bring blankets! And let the doctor know we're on our way." He kissed me. "You have a habit of finding trouble. Is this what I have to look forward to in the future?"

"I certainly hope not," I said. "But I wouldn't hold my breath if I were you."

"I thought I lost you, Nicole. I thought...I can't lose you. I love you, Nic." He pressed his forehead against mine, his breath slow and deep. "I love you."

I closed my eyes and inhaled the scent of him, earthy, woodsy, with the brightest hint of verbena. "I love you too."

CHAPTER 23

*F*ive weeks after we'd turned in our official report on the take-down of the Little Piggy killer and the exposure of illegal arms deals coming out of Fort Leonard Wood, Dom and I were awarded commendations for excellence. We were given a week off from work to recover from the ordeal. Dom agreed we should spend it in Peculiar with my folks. Eldin kept me informed on the excavations around the TSS compound and Judge Holts home. They'd found more bodies. Over a dozen. The thought of how long he'd been operating in and around of Peculiar made me sick, but I was contented, knowing we'd stopped him from ever hurting another person.

It was good to be home again with all of us safe and healthy for a normal vacation with no killer track down.

"You look beautiful, sweetheart," my mom said. "I love your new hairstyle."

"Thanks, mom." I didn't tell her that I'd had it cut because Judge Holt had snatched chunks of it from my head and made it seriously uneven. I still had nightmares about his eyes sometimes, but waking up in Dom's arms gave the bad dreams less power.

"What are those two doing back there?" I asked. Dom and my dad had gone back to Dad's office, shortly after we'd arrived home, and they hadn't come out for over thirty minutes.

Mom shrugged. "Who knows with men? Come into the kitchen. I've made cheesecake."

"Yes, definitely, yes." I followed Mom. "Do you have Earl Grey tea?"

"Of course," she said as if I'd insulted her. "It pairs perfectly with cheesecake. I taught you that."

I grinned and flexed my shoulder. It was still stiff, but it and my ankle had healed. The bullet scar had given me a ton of street cred with the other agents.

"It's so good to have you home, Puddin'."

"It sure is," my dad said, as he in Dom finally joined us. My man looked so handsome. I really did love looking at his face.

"What in the heck were you two up to back there?"

"I had a few things I had to straighten out with your dad," Dom said.

I thought they'd straightened out all their differences weeks ago. "What are you talking about?"

My dad nodded. "Go ahead, son. You have my permission."

"Permission for what?" I asked.

Dom went to the refrigerator and pulled out a parfait cup with chocolate pudding in it. He dropped down on one knee in front of me, and I stopped breathing as my heart caught in my throat. Too dumbstruck to speak, I looked at my parents. My mom clutched imaginary pearls at her chest, and Dad was grinning like an insane person.

Dom, however, had the most serious expression on his face and his hands shook as he held the pudding cup. On top of the soft-set dessert was a square cut diamond ring with a channel of smaller diamonds around it in a platinum setting. "It's beautiful," I whispered, my voice hoarse with emotion.

"Nicole Rae Taylor, you are the best thing that has ever happened to me in my life. I love you more than I ever thought it was possible to love anyone. When I think of the future, I can't imagine it without you by my side. I will support you and love you always. I will be the partner you deserve. These are the promises I make to you if you agree to be my wife."

My hand trembled as I held it out for him, and he put the ring in his mouth to lick off the excess pudding then placed it on my right ring finger.

"Is that a yes, Puddin'?" he asked.

"Yes," I said. "It's a yes!"

Dom stood up and lifted me from the floor and swung me around.

A cork popped behind me and champagne sprayed the kitchen. My mom held the overflowing bottle and had four flutes ready to go. She smiled. "Champagne goes well with cheesecake too."

The End

MY WOLFY WEDDING - CHAPTER ONE

Peculiar Mysteries Book 8

Billy Bob Smith and Chavvah Trimmel cordially request the honor of your presence on their happy (disastrous) day. To celebrate

(survive) their union on Friday, the Twenty-First of December, Two Thousand Eighteen at Four-Twenty-Three p.m.
  Destination: Peculiar, Missouri.

The only thing Chavvah wants more than to marry Billy Bob is to have his baby, but since that ship has sailed thanks to prior trauma, she's happy just to get him down the aisle. The date is set for the Winter Solstice, marking the longest night of year, but a challenge from an unexpected guest, is turning her special day into a fight-club nightmare. And after having postponed the wedding twice already, Chav is starting to think fate hates her guts.

On top of that, there are almost forty werewolves camped out on Billy Bob's property, claiming that Chav and Billy Bob are their new leaders. But when Chav tries to get her spirit guide, Brother Wolf, to cough up answers, he ignores her. Worst, the silent deity is sending her BFF Sunny visions that are taking a physical toll on her human friend's all too frail body.

Throw in Billy Bob's manipulative father, Chav's pushy mother, and other surprise guests, these two furry lovebirds may never make it to "I do!"

Available at All Your Favorite eTailers

Chapter One

December 19^{*th*}*, Two days before my wedding date...*

"The weather man is calling for mild temperatures this entire week," Sunny said. "High forties to mid fifties. It looks like you're going to have an unseasonably warm winter nuptial, Chav. Isn't that good news?" She clapped her hands and danced around me. Dawn and Jude, my adorable nephew and niece, giggled at their mother's antics.

"I don't need a white wedding," I told her. Though I really wanted one. The idea of getting married under fairy lights in a blanket of snow, against the contrast of red roses and carnations made my inner princess squee. Doc had agreed to wear a white tux, but I'd had to suffer through a little razzing from all my friends about how girly I was getting. Frankly, I didn't give a crap. I was marrying the wolf of my dreams in less than a week. Nothing and no one was going to put a damper on my great mood.

My phone, sitting on the counter near the coffee pot, beeped. I walked over and looked down at the text.

"No," I said, unable to keep the horror from my tone.

"What is it?" Sunny asked.

I held up the phone for her to see. She gasped.

I seconded that emotion.

The text was from my mother, and it only contained three words. *On my way.* I cast an accusatory glance at Sunny. "Who told her?"

"Not me." Her expression mirrored my horror. "Your mother has a way of ruining a perfectly good wedding."

"You mean, she has a way of trying to put an end to a

perfectly good wedding." She wasn't happy about my engagement to Billy Bob Smith, a pure lycanthrope, and the only one of his kind in this area. "She still thinks that werewolves are violent rogues who have no self-control."

Sunny snorted. "I've been in the other room when you two are having sex. I don't think she's wrong about that self-control thing."

I laughed. "Well, he's certainly not violent."

Sunny nodded. "Not any more than anybody else in this town."

"Besides, I can shift into a wolf now, so I don't understand what her deal is. We're part-flippin-werewolf" Recently I'd discovered I could shift into either wolf or coyote depending on my mood. According Billy Bob, I was one of a kind. I shook my head as I pictured my mother's reaction to the news of my tri-nature, and how my ancestral heritage made all the lycanthrope bigotry complete and utter bullshit. "The family vendetta was a complete lie. Why can't she just give it up?"

"I've got no answers, Chav. I gave her two grandchildren, and, still, she barely tolerates me."

"Mom doesn't hate you."

Sunny snorted again.

"Well, not as much as she hates Billy Bob."

"That's probably true. She even tried to get me to side with her at Thanksgiving."

I raised my brow at her. "You ate Thanksgiving with me."

"On the phone," she confessed.

"Oh."

"Don't worry. I totally had your back. I told her that there wasn't enough BFF ju-ju in this world that could pry your legs from around that man's waist."

"Sunny!" My face flamed with heat. "You didn't."

She shrugged. "I might not have used those exact words, but something to that effect. As the saying goes, the va-jay-jay wants what the va-jay-jay wants."

"That's not how the saying goes." A knock at the door rescued me from the deteriorating conversation.

Sunny smiled. "That's probably her now."

I groaned. "Damn it." I left Sunny, who wasn't eager to see my mom either, in the kitchen as I walked through the living room to the front door. I braced myself for the ill-wind blowing in and opened the door just as another knock occurred.

My mother was not on the others side of the door. Instead, an extremely tall, lanky gentleman with short silver hair, gray-blue eyes, and golden skin. There were fine lines around his eyes that marked him as an elder.

"Can I help you?"

"Is William home?"

"Who?"

The man looked surprised. "William Smith."

"Billy Bob?"

The guy nodded, his expression full of disapproval. "Yes, him."

"He's not home right now." Normally, Billy Bob worked at the clinic during the daytime hours. Today, however, he was getting fitted for his tux, along with his best men Brady Corman, Babe, and Ed Thompson. "Can I give him a message?"

The man hemmed and hawed for a moment then finally said, "Yes." He cast me a steely stare. "Tell him his father is in town, and I'd like to see him at his earliest convenience."

I returned a suspicious gaze. "Does he know how to contact you?"

The man pulled his wallet from his back pocket and produced a card. William Robert Smith, Sr. Smith Contractors, LLC, and a business number along with a mobile phone number. Mister Smith handed me the card and said, "He can call me on my cell phone."

I took the card and saluted with it. "I'll give him the message."

"Can I ask you a question?"

I shrugged. "Sure."

"Who are you?"

I knew enough not to be hurt that Billy Bob's dad had no idea who I was or what I meant to his son. The doc told me once he hadn't spoken to his father in over fifteen years. He hadn't elaborated, and I hadn't pried. Now, as I studied the man, who really didn't look much like my mate at all, I kind of wished I would have—pried, that is. "I'm his...girlfriend," I finally said. Not a lie, but not the whole truth. I didn't know if Billy Bob wanted his dad crashing our festivities. I know I sure didn't want my mom there.

"Is this his house or yours?" he asked.

"That's two questions." I smiled to soften my words.

"It is," he agreed. "My apologies. Please give the message to William. Tell him I don't like to be kept waiting."

And Doc doesn't like to be bossed. I crossed my arms as irritation replaced my curiosity. It was no wonder Billy Bob left home and never looked back.

"Chav?" Sunny asked when she walked into the living room. "Are you okay?"

William Smith turned his gaze to my friend. His eyes were that of a pure predator. "She's human." Even though he was staring at her, he addressed me. His accusation surprised me because there wasn't any way to tell if someone was therian or human based on looking at them or even by scent. "I thought this place was a therianthrope haven." The little growl in his voice raised the hairs on the back of my neck.

His demeanor pushed my animal to the surface, and I think William was a surprised as me to find it was wolf, not coyote, who challenged him.

"There are no other lycanthropes in this territory. What tribe are you from?" His interest had turned back to me and away from Sunny.

I let out a slow breath forcing my wolf to retreat. "I'll let the doc know you stopped by." Since he still stood just outside on the porch, I took a step forward, my hand on the door, closing it between us. I turned to Sunny.

She ran a hand through her short, blonde hair. "Looks like your mom isn't the only parental wedding crasher. Mister Smith seems like a real sweetheart."

I walked over to window and peeked behind the

curtain. A truck pulled back up then took off down the driveway toward the one road in and out of town.

"I've got a bad feeling about that one."

Sunny put her hand on my shoulder. "Hey, you can't have the psychic gig. It's the only thing I got going for me. You know, aside from saggy milk sacks and crow's feet."

"There's always plastic surgery. I hear they're doing amazing things with stem cell therapy. You don't even have to go under a knife for that."

"Mean," Sunny said. Her lower lip jutted in a fake pout. "Seriously though, does that stem cell stuff work, because…"

"Oh, stop it. You're beautiful. And I have it on good authority that your husband adores you just the way you are."

"I know. I'm just working on a contingency plan. You know, for the future." Sunny wrapped her arms around me, and for a human, she gave the most spine crushing hugs of anyone I'd ever met.

Frankly, it was just what I needed. "I don't know what I'd do without you."

"Good thing you don't have to. You're stuck with me, darling." She unclenched her arms from around me. "I better go though. Michele Thompson has a date tonight, and I promised I'd be home before four so she could get cleaned up for it."

"Jo Jo?" I asked. Jo Jo Corman, a twenty-one-year-old coyote shifter who'd been working for Sunny and me at Sunny's Outlook for nearly three years had a real thing for Michele. They'd dated before, but the girl could be fickle.

"I didn't ask, and she didn't volunteer," Sunny said. "But Jo Jo finally shaved the scruff off his face and got a new haircut yesterday." She picked up her purse and gave me another quick hug. "I'll see you tonight."

PARANORMAL MYSTERIES & ROMANCES

By Renee George

Nora Black Midlife Psychic Mysteries

www.norablackmysteries.com
Sense & Scent Ability (Book 1)
For Whom the Smell Tolls (Book 2)
War of the Noses (Book 3)
Aroma With A View (Book 4) Coming in 2021

Peculiar Mysteries

www.peculiarmysteries.com
You've Got Tail (Book 1) FREE Download
My Furry Valentine (Book 2)
Thank You For Not Shifting (Book 3)
My Hairy Halloween (Book 4)
In the Midnight Howl (Book 5)
My Peculiar Road Trip (Magic & Mayhem) (Book 6)
Furred Lines (Book7)
My Wolfy Wedding (Book 8)
Who Let The Wolves Out? (Book 9)

My Thanksgiving Faux Paw (Book 10)

Witchin' Impossible Cozy Mysteries

www.witchinimpossible.com
Witchin' Impossible (Book 1)
Rogue Coven (Book 2)
Familiar Protocol (Booke 3)
Mr & Mrs. Shift (Book 4)

Barkside of the Moon Mysteries

www.barksideofthemoonmysteries.com
Pit Perfect Murder (Book 1)
Murder & The Money Pit (Book 2)
The Pit List Murders (Book 3)
Pit & Miss Murder (Book 4)
The Prune Pit Murder (Book 5)

Madder Than Hell

www.madder-than-hell.com
Gone With The Minion (Book 1)
Devil On A Hot Tin Roof (Book 2)
A Street Car Named Demonic (Book 3)

Hex Drive

https://www.renee-george.com/hex-drive-series
Hex Me, Baby, One More Time (Book 1)
Oops, I Hexed It Again (Book 2)
I Want Your Hex (Book 3)
Hex Me With Your Best Shot (Book 4)

Midnight Shifters

www.midnightshifters.com

Midnight Shift (Book 1)

The Bear Witch Project (Book 2)

A Door to Midnight (Book 3)

A Shade of Midnight (Book 4)

Midnight Before Christmas (Book 5)

ABOUT THE AUTHOR

I am a USA Today Bestselling author who writes para-normal mysteries and romances because I love all things whodunit, Otherworldly, and weird. Also, I wish my pittie, the adorable Kona Princess Warrior, and my beagle, Josie the Incontinent Princess, could talk. Or at least be more like Scooby-Doo and help me unmask villains at the haunted house up the street.

When I'm not writing about mystery-solving were-cougars or the adventures of a hapless psychic living among shapeshifters, I am preyed upon by stray kittens who end up living in my house because I can't say no to those sweet, furry faces. (Someone stop telling them where I live!)

I live in Mid-Missouri with my family and I spend my non-writing time doing really cool stuff...like watching TV and cleaning up dog poop.

Join My Newsletter

Follow Me On Bookbub!

www.ingramcontent.com/pod-product-compliance
Lightning Source LLC
Chambersburg PA
CBHW051454170626
46811CB00002B/479